THE PECULIAR POWER OF TABITHA BROWN

Mary Hooper knows more than most people what makes a good story – she's had over six hundred published in teenage and women's magazines, from *Just Seventeen* to *Woman's Own*, and she has taught evening classes in Creative Writing. In addition, she's the highly-regarded author of over thirty titles for young people, including *The Boyfriend Trap, Mad About the Boy, The Great Twin Trick, Spook Spotting* and *Spooks Ahoy!*

Books by the same author

Best Friends, Worst Luck
The Boyfriend Trap
Mad About the Boy
Spook Spotting
Spooks Ahoy!

THE PECULIAR POWER OF TABITHA BROWN

MARY HOOPER

WALKER BOOKS
AND SUBSIDIARIES

LONDON • BOSTON • SYDNEY

First published 1998 by Walker Books Ltd
87 Vauxhall Walk, London SE11 5HJ

This edition published 1999

2 4 6 8 10 9 7 5 3 1

Text © 1998 Mary Hooper
Cover illustration © 1998 Barry Jones

This book has been typeset in Sabon.

Printed in Great Britain by Cox & Wyman Ltd,
Reading, Berkshire

British Library Cataloguing in Publication Data
A catalogue record for this book is available from
the British Library.

ISBN 0-7445-6399-2

CHAPTER ONE

Everyone knew, of course, that there was something odd about Aunt Mitzi.

On the way home from our visit there last summer, my brother Sam called her dippy-doo-da and Jamie, who's his twin, said she was as mad as a balloon. When they said that, Mum didn't tell them off, she just laughed. And Dad was just as bad – he referred to her as "one of the barmy aunts" and made a fuss if Mum ever wanted to go there, finding all sorts of reasons why he was too busy.

Aunt Mitzi was Granny's sister and Mum's aunt, so really our great-aunt. We didn't see a lot of her because, apart from the fact that she was batty, she lived in Somerset and we live in the Midlands, so it took hours to get there. She never forgot my birthday, though, and there was always a card at Christmas. It usually had a black cat on it.

I remember her coming to a family wedding once wearing a black droopy dress down to her ankles and a strange sort of feathery hat with a veil over one eye, and everyone had talked about her behind her back. The other time I remember seeing her was when some cousin or other went off to Australia, and she arrived at our house for the leaving party a week after he'd gone.

I suppose it was just lucky, really, that we happened to go down to see her last summer, about a year before she died. Dad had to go to some business meeting in Somerset, we were well into school holidays, and Mum said it was a golden opportunity and we might never see the old dear again.

We drove for three hours in the car, then Dad got out at Taunton and Mum took over at the wheel. A bit after that we were driving along the dual carriageway and Mum was trying to remember where to turn off to get onto the right small coast road.

Sam and Jamie were fighting, scuffling and arguing, and I was getting really fed up. This isn't unusual – they're always fighting and I'm always fed up with them – but this time it was worse because I'd been stuck in the back of the car between them, so was getting poked and shoved and bickered at on both sides. I was trying very hard not to lose my temper, though, because whenever I did that I just saw red, scratched, screamed and ended up completely in the wrong.

"Boys, do try not to roll all over Tabitha," Mum did bother to say once, and, "Tabitha, don't let them get to you," but other than that she just ignored them, as usual. Mum has this policy of keeping her distance and "letting us get on with it" which, as far as I can see, just means letting the twins get on with whatever they like, be it grievous bodily harm or whatever.

To tell the truth, none of us three was really bothered about seeing Aunt Mitzi. I wanted to go round some interesting shops I'd glimpsed in the nearby town, Sam wanted to go on the beach and kick a ball about and Jamie had brought a selection of cars and just wanted to roll them around somewhere.

"Almost there!" Mum suddenly shouted over her shoulder.

I gave a squeal of relief.

"You can just say polite hellos to Aunt Mitzi, have something to eat and then go off and do your own thing."

"I can't do my own thing," I objected, "because there aren't any shops round here."

"No, I don't mean you," Mum said. "The boys can go off exploring or whatever, but I want you to stop and keep me company." She smiled at me in the driving mirror. "Aunt Mitzi's very fond of you."

I'd been told this before: that I took after Aunt Mitzi, that I'd inherited her looks and all that (and her *temper*, Mum had told me on more than one occasion).

The twins both pulled faces at me – sort of "get you" faces.

"She's an old witch and she's going to lock you away and keep you there for ever," Sam hissed.

"No, she's not," I said, "but she *is* very old and because she likes me, when she dies she's going to leave me a lot of money."

He thought for a moment, then he said to Mum, "Can I stay and keep you company, too?"

Mum shook her head, peering along the row of bungalows we were passing. "You'd be much too noisy. She's only got a very small place. Besides, Aunt Mitzi's not keen on boys."

"See!" I smiled triumphantly at Sam.

"We're only going to be here a couple of hours anyway. And then we'll collect Dad and have a nice meal on the way home." She pulled up alongside a flowery hedge. "Here we are. Aunt Mitzi's."

We peered in over the hedge and through the broken-down gate towards the funny little house.

"Is this where she lives? It's like a railway carriage!" Jamie said.

Sam gave a guffaw of laughter. "She lives in a train!"

"I think it might have been, once," Mum said.

"Was there ever an Uncle Mitzi?" I asked.

Mum said no, there wasn't. "Aunt Mitzi isn't the marrying kind." She switched off the engine. "She likes being alone. Always has done."

The grass in the front garden was long and floppy. It was so long we could hardly get the gate open. There were a lot of rose bushes overhanging the path and their flowers had dropped, covering the mossy slabs with pink, white and red. Walking through the gate, I pretended I was the Queen of Sheba and someone had strewn the petals across my path.

Sam looked at me. "Why have you got that stupid look on your face?"

"Nah! That's what she normally looks like!" Jamie hooted.

"Tabitha Brown went to town, with her knickers hanging down!" Sam chanted.

This, a particular favourite of theirs, demonstrates not only what I'm up against, but also the general level of their humour.

"Oh, do shut up!" I said.

Sam started whispering to Jamie and they both snorted with laughter. They were obviously planning something; it was the only time they ever went quiet.

11

"Don't you start!" Mum warned, looking at each of us in turn. *Each of us*, I thought, when I hadn't done a thing apart from be there. "I want a quiet and civilized visit. I want Aunt Mitzi to see what nice children I've got."

"You'd better leave those two in the car, then," I said.

Mum tapped at the front door, which was painted green and had a slide-down window, exactly like the door of an old-fashioned railway carriage. Sam said, "All aboard the 6.20!"

"Hold very tight, please!" Jamie added.

"Hold tight to your knickers!" Sam said, and they both collapsed with laughter.

I turned my back on them and we waited, but Aunt Mitzi didn't appear. I tried to look through the lace curtain behind the door but couldn't see anything. I wondered if, inside, there would be emergency cords to pull above the windows, and NO SMOKING notices, and if the loo would be like the loo on a train, with signs saying PLEASE DO NOT FLUSH AT THE STATION.

"Does she know we're coming?" Sam asked, and Mum said she'd written to Aunt Mitzi two weeks ago *and* given her a ring to confirm.

"I'm sure she'll be around somewhere," she said. She held up the cool-box she'd brought. "I think we'll go into the back garden and eat

12

our sandwiches, and by the time we've done that she may have appeared."

"Why did you bring sandwiches?" I asked. "Couldn't she give us something to eat?"

Mum rolled her eyes. "Sam only likes egg. Jamie only likes Marmite. You only like cheese."

I nodded. This was true.

"Besides, I don't think Aunt Mitzi eats much and we don't want to impose. She probably makes a loaf last her a week."

The boys had disappeared around the back and Mum followed them. I heard Sam yell, "There's an outside loo!"

"I wanna use it first!" Jamie shouted, and then there was a scuffle and the noise of a door being wrenched off its hinges. Mum's footsteps quickened to get to them.

I peered through the front window again – or tried to, feeling hot and bothered. The journey had been long and boring and it would be ridiculous if we had to go home again without seeing Aunt Mitzi, especially as I'd told my friend Emily about this eccentric relative of mine. I was hoping to be able to report some interesting dottiness. (Emily is quite interesting in her own right, you see, being a brilliant dancer who will probably end up in ballet school.)

I turned away from the window and was about to follow Mum round the back when

13

my attention was caught by something black in the garden. I went closer: it was a cat, curled up into a perfect circle, asleep in the middle of a clump of blue flowers.

I bent down and stroked it. I've always wanted a cat, but Jamie and Sam have Mutton, an awful, smelly old dog that was given to them by the man next door when he moved, so I've never been allowed to have one. This, I reckon, is another example of acute unfairness in our family.

As I stroked it, the cat's fur shivered slightly, but it didn't wake up.

"Puss … puss … puss," I said, as I tickled round its head and down the curve of its spine. "Are you Aunt Mitzi's cat?" I asked. I know this was pretty stupid of me and I wouldn't normally admit to having asked a cat a question, except that when I said it, the cat suddenly put its head up.

It looked me over and then it sat up slowly. It was very sleek and shiny, with slitty green eyes. Sitting there amid the flowers it looked stately and elegant – like one of those Egyptian cats you see made into china table lamps.

"You're a beauty, aren't you?" I said, and the cat blinked as if acknowledging my interest but saying that it was no more than was due to it.

It yawned, showing a perfect pink tongue and sharp white teeth, and then it stretched along its length, straightening its front legs so that its paws divided into individual toes and showed little white claws.

I stood up. "Are you coming round the back?" I said, for I'd suddenly decided I was starving. "Come and see what sandwiches we've got. Nice fishy ones!" I lied.

I walked away, calling "Puss … puss …" under my breath, but the cat just sat and looked, quietly and consideringly, as if weighing me up.

I went round the back, to where Mum had settled herself under a tree. "There's a cat in the front garden. Has Aunt Mitzi got a cat?" I asked.

"I'm not sure," she said. "I *do* seem to remember seeing one once – but it can't be the same one, because that was years ago."

"Was it black?" I asked.

Mum nodded. "But I don't think she can have a cat now, because she's always travelling around."

"What d'you mean?" I asked. "Does she go to foreign countries?"

"Oh, no." Mum shook her head. "I just mean she walks – walks miles, right across the country, and a cat would be a bit of a tie."

"Cats are better than dogs for leaving on their own." I never lost an opportunity to promote the advantages of owning one. "I bet Mutton's chewed up half the kitchen by the time we get home."

I looked down the garden. It was narrow and very long. In fact, I'd never seen such a garden, with so many trees and shrubs that you couldn't see where it ended and the next one began.

"Where d'you think she is, then?" I asked.

But Mum wasn't really listening, she was looking across to where Sam and Jamie were hanging off trees and bellowing. "Those boys!" she said, in the fond voice she keeps for the twins.

"Can't we knock at the neighbours or something and ask them where she is?" I urged. "We don't want to go all the way home without having seen her, do we?"

"Pity we haven't got a few more trees in our garden at home," said Mum.

I nodded towards the railway carriage house. "You don't think she's in there …" I lowered my voice, "… dead, or something?"

Mum forgot about the twins and followed my gaze. "No, of course not. She's probably gone out shopping."

"But there aren't any shops."

"Well, perhaps she's visiting someone or…"

At that moment Aunt Mitzi came round the corner. She was tall and thin and wearing a dark cotton dress. She had black hair, greying at the edges, caught up in a knot on the top of her head. She walked slowly, elegantly, and when she reached us she smiled slightly, looking straight at me. She was quite old, very wrinkled, but she had sharp, sparkly green eyes.

"I am so sorry, my dears," she said, "I was unavoidably delayed."

CHAPTER TWO

An hour or so later I was bored. We'd eaten all the sandwiches, Jamie and Sam had gone exploring, and Mum and Aunt Mitzi were still sitting in the garden talking about dead uncles and various stray cousins.

I'd already revisited the front garden hoping to find the cat, but had found only an empty space inside the clump of blue flowers: a nest of trodden-down stalks.

I went right down to the end of the garden, very slowly, calling "Puss … puss…" under my breath, but no one came. It was very hot, very still. There weren't any birds singing. Perhaps they knew that a cat lived there.

I went back to Mum and Aunt Mitzi but they were still talking and I couldn't get a word in. As there wasn't a loo indoors I'd already visited the outside one twice, just for something to do, and was thinking about going again, when there was a pause in the conversation.

"I saw a cat earlier!" I said to Aunt Mitzi quickly, before they started again. "A nice black cat in the front garden. Does it belong to you?"

Aunt Mitzi looked at me gravely and shook her head. "Cats don't belong to anyone," she said. "They sometimes stay a while, if it suits them."

"Well, is … er … that one staying with you?"

She hesitated a moment. "It's here sometimes," she said a bit mysteriously.

I felt vaguely annoyed. Why couldn't she give proper answers? Either she had a cat, or she didn't.

"It's not here at the moment," she added.

"Well, it was earlier," I said, and I think I must have sounded a bit abrupt because Mum said quickly that she thought she'd remembered a cat here once before, years ago. "But of course it couldn't be the same one," she added.

Aunt Mitzi nodded and smiled. "The black cat comes and goes," she said, and I stored this up as being dotty enough to repeat to Emily.

"Tabitha loves cats," Mum said chattily. "She was always hanging out of the pram looking for them when she was a baby."

Aunt Mitzi smiled into the distance. "Ah, you were a very beautiful baby, Tabitha."

I smiled politely; I never think it counts when relatives say you're beautiful.

"I remember you had thick black hair even when you were quite tiny."

"Did you see me when I was a really small baby, then?" I asked.

"Yes, I did," Aunt Mitzi said solemnly. "I came to the hospital when you were only hours old."

Mum nodded at me. "I've told you before, haven't I? You were quite a big deal. One of the first girls to be born in the family for ages."

"Truly one of us…" Aunt Mitzi murmured.

There was something about the way she said it – it seemed to mean more than just one of the family. "What's that mean?" I asked.

"One of us. Well…" Aunt Mitzi faltered, and then she just looked at me as if she wanted to say, *Don't you know?*

But I didn't.

"I expect Aunt Mitzi just means your black hair and your green eyes," Mum put in.

"Of course," said Aunt Mitzi. "You look like my grandmother. And my mother, of course – your mum's granny. She was very beautiful, even when she was old. She had a marvellous creamy skin, green eyes and jet-black hair."

Aunt Mitzi's voice faded and she stared into the distance.

"Yes?" I prompted her, because it was

getting interesting. "And what else?"

"Well, she married a rich man and had fourteen children," Aunt Mitzi went on, "twelve boys and two girls: me and your granny. But out of all those children, I was the only one who took after her in looks and temperament."

"Then when Aunt Mitzi's brothers – my uncles – married they all seemed to have boys," Mum said.

Aunt Mitzi turned to her. "And even though you were a very pretty baby, you still weren't quite one of us," she said, touching Mum's reddish-brown hair.

"No, that colouring skipped a generation and didn't appear again until you came along, Tabitha," said Mum.

"So I'm special, am I?" I said, and added pointedly, "though not as special as the *twins*, I don't suppose." I said this because I'd had years of hanging onto the pram and pushchair handles while people cooed over them and ignored me.

"You, my dear, are *very* special," said Aunt Mitzi solemnly.

There was another lull in the conversation. "D'you think I could have a glass of water?" I asked, because I was dying to see inside the railway carriage and Mum was probably going to announce that we were going home any minute.

"Of course," Aunt Mitzi said, "let's go in."

As she stood up I thought to myself that her face was old, but not her movements. She moved gracefully and she didn't make puffing noises or clutch at her back like my gran did.

We went inside, but actually it wasn't that thrilling. I'd been hoping that it would be like an old-fashioned railway carriage: all plush, buttoned upholstery and little gold gas lamps, but it was just a neat little kitchen with an ordinary small sitting-room leading off it. There were no PLEASE DO NOT notices at all.

Mum came in, too, and looked round. "Just as I remembered," she said.

"It suits me," said Aunt Mitzi. "I don't like change."

She got me a glass of water from the deep, white sink in the kitchen. I drank half and, while Mum was examining some herbs on the windowsill, wandered into the sitting-room and went to sit down on a dining-room chair.

"Don't!" Aunt Mitzi said. "That's where the cat sits."

"Oh," I said. So she *did* have a cat. She'd practically told me she didn't. I looked down at the chair. It had a hard leather seat, but on it had been placed a red cushion. It was a rather grand cushion for a cat: thick velvet with gold and red piping around the edges, and it had a cat-shaped dent in the centre of it. When I touched it some black fur came off on my fingers.

"Is he around?" I asked.

"She," said Aunt Mitzi. "Is *she* around."

"Is she around?" I asked obediently.

Aunt Mitzi shook her head, looking at me quizzically. "Not at the moment, no."

"Does he – she – have a name?"

"No," said Aunt Mitzi.

"So how do you call her?"

"I don't," Aunt Mitzi said.

Jamie and Sam often spoke like this, just to be difficult, but because it was Aunt Mitzi speaking it wasn't so much irritating as intriguing. There was something about the way she spoke and the way she looked at me with those crinkly, bright green eyes; it was as if she was really saying something else, something hidden, that I had to puzzle out.

"Will she come in for her tea before we go?"

"No," Aunt Mitzi said, and I remember wondering how she could know that so definitely when cats usually please themselves whether they're going to come in or not.

"I like cats," I said.

"I know," said Aunt Mitzi. She smiled that strange smile again. "I think people are two types, don't you? They're cat people or dog people. That's how I define everyone."

"Mmmm," I said vaguely, storing this up as another example of dottiness for Emily.

And though I looked for it everywhere, I didn't see the cat again before we went home.

CHAPTER THREE

And I didn't see Aunt Mitzi again, either. Not ever, because she died a year after that visit. I felt a bit sad when I heard, but not that much because I hardly knew her. I did wonder who was going to look after the cat, though.

In spite of me being "one of us" and all that business, I didn't go to the funeral. It was on a Thursday right at the end of summer term and was only a "very small affair", Mum said. She and Dad went there and back on the same day and Mrs Neil-next-door kept an eye on the twins after school. Originally Mrs Neil-next-door was supposed to keep an eye on me, too, but seeing as I couldn't stand her, I'd made arrangements to go home with Emily.

As soon as we got in from school Emily did ballet exercises at the barre she's got in her room, and when she'd finished that we just flopped about reading magazines. Later we got to talking about what Aunt Mitzi's funeral might be like, whether there would be a reading of the will, who was going to look after the cat and – especially – who she would leave the little railway carriage house to.

"You don't think it'll be you, do you?" Emily asked excitedly.

"Might be," I said, because if it wasn't me – so special and "one of us" – who *was* it going to be?

"That'll be all right," Emily said. "We can go down there in the holidays."

We talked about this for a bit and whether we'd get the same school holidays when she got her scholarship and went away, and then we had tea (proper sit-up-at-table tea – her mum is like that) and I went home.

The twins were being fed at Mrs Neil-next-door's so I had a nice, peaceful hour to myself before Mum and Dad came in. I went to laze about in my room a bit.

My room's OK, but it's really small – the smallest room in the house apart from the loo. If I had a bigger one I'd paint a mural on the wall and have lots of ethnic-type hangings and a proper desk. As it is, I've done the best I can: hanging over the bed I've got a coloured-silk tent affair made out of a sari I got from a jumble sale, and I've draped purple scarves over the table lamps.

About seven o'clock Mum and Dad came in.

I ran downstairs and looked for a pet carrier, but there was no sign of one, so the mysterious black cat obviously hadn't been left to me. A minute later the twins appeared, the awful Mutton leaping about at their side.

"What was it like?" Jamie demanded.

"Why is it called a *fun*eral," Sam asked, "when it's not fun?"

"I really don't know," Mum said, putting the kettle on.

Mutton leaped at me, putting muddy paws all down the front of my jeans and slobbering his wet mouth on me. I pushed him off.

"Were there many people there?" I asked.

"About twenty, I suppose," Mum said. "The neighbours and a few uncles I haven't seen for ages, and two of my cousins – both of them much older and fatter. I only ever seem to see my family at weddings and funerals now," she added, shaking her head.

"Is there any exciting news, then?" I asked.

"Well, your cousin Julia is doing fine – she's due to have the baby next month. And Peter's son is living in Japan now."

I nodded absently. "Was there a will reading?" I asked.

Dad puffed out his cheeks. "A will! She didn't have anything worth leaving."

"What about the house?"

"It was rented," said Mum.

"Oh," I said. So much for that, then.

Jamie and Sam were scuffling in a corner and Mutton was giving short barks of excitement, leaping from one to the other. "What *are* you fighting about now?" Mum asked. "I hope you weren't like this at Mrs Neil's."

"Did you go back to Aunt Mitzi's house?" I asked Mum.

"Only briefly," she said. "We had tea and cakes in the cottage next door and just popped back to Aunt Mitzi's for ... for something." She and Dad grinned at each other.

"What about the cat, though? Who's looking after it?"

"Oh, that cat!" Dad said. "I remember that cat. It once scratched me when I sat on its chair."

"That was *years* ago," Mum said. "It can't have been the same cat – not the one that Tabitha saw last time we went."

"So did you see *that* one *this* time?" I asked impatiently. "Who's looking after it?"

Mum shrugged: she didn't know. "It must belong to a neighbour or something. I don't think it was Aunt Mitzi's own."

"Well, what about all Aunt Mitzi's furniture and everything? And all her clothes? What will happen to that sort of stuff?"

"Uncle John lives quite close and he'll sort all that out," Mum said. "There's really nothing of any worth there. No jewellery or anything." She and Dad looked at each other again. "She did leave *you* something, though, Tabitha."

Dad smirked. "Something *very* nice."

"Don't tease her!" Mum said.

The twins suddenly stopped what they were doing.

"What did she get left?" Sam asked.

"Is it precious?" Jamie said. "Is it gold coins?"

Mum bent down and picked up the large plastic carrier bag she'd come in with. "Well, it was obviously precious to Aunt Mitzi," she said.

"Why haven't we got anything?" Sam complained.

"Tab always gets the good things..." Jamie whined.

Mum pushed the bag across the table to me. "Here you are, love. This is what she wanted you to have. Don't get too excited."

Well, of course I couldn't help getting a *bit* excited, thinking it might be letters, perhaps, or a special dress, or an antique of some sort. With everyone's eyes on me, I opened the carrier and pulled out what was inside – and was really disappointed. And, despite the fact that she was dead, I got a bit cross with Aunt Mitzi for setting me up.

The twins started hooting with laughter.

"It's a bit of crummy old material!" Jamie jeered.

"It's an old cushion!" Sam said.

He was right. It *was* a cushion. The cat's cushion.

I rolled my eyes at Mum. "Why has she sent me this?"

"I really don't know."

Dad made a loopy gesture with his hand. "Barking, of course," he said. "What do you expect?"

Jamie made a noise like a dog howling. Mutton joined in.

"Sshh," Mum said. "Perhaps it's packed with fivers."

"Tabitha Brown went to town, with a cushion…" Jamie began, but couldn't finish.

I stroked the velvet cushion thoughtfully, as if I was stroking the cat. "I'd rather have had the cat," I said. "I wonder why she didn't leave me him. *Her*."

"Well, if she didn't own the cat she could hardly leave it to you," Mum said.

"We don't want no crummy cats here," Jamie said. "Mutton *hates* cats."

"Who told you she'd left me the cushion?" I asked.

"The woman next door – where we had tea. She said Aunt Mitzi had specifically said you, her great-niece, Tabitha Brown, were to have the cushion and to tell you that…" She looked at Dad. "What were the exact words?"

"To tell you that her nine lives were up,"

Dad said. He looked at the boys. "Your mother's family, eh?" he said. "Off their trolleys!"

Talk about giving them encouragement. The twins fell about, sniggering.

Sam suddenly leant across me and grabbed the cushion. "Mutton can have it!" he said. "It can go in his basket."

I snatched it back. "Oh, no, it can't!"

"Children!" Mum said warningly.

"Cat's cushion! Fancy being left a cat's cushion!" Sam said, dancing around me and making grabs at it.

I ignored him. Well, I tried to, but he was dancing in this really stupid way, so I reached out to flick him round the ear and somehow managed to scratch his cheek.

He immediately let out a mighty yell and Mum rushed over to him.

"I'm off," Dad said, picking up the newspaper and leaving the room.

"Tabitha!" Mum said in a shocked voice. "There's a long scratch. You've broken the skin. He's bleeding!"

"I didn't *mean* to do it," I said sullenly.

"It's pouring with blood!" Jamie said. "You could sign your name in it."

"It's not pouring!" I said. "You can hardly see it."

Sam carried on whinging.

"Oh, let him have the cushion, for goodness'

sake," said Mum.

I felt my temper beginning to rise. "But it's mine!"

"He only wants to look at it," said Mum, and as she spoke, Sam recovered from his mortal wound enough to snatch the cushion again. I went to grab it back but he threw it over my head to Jamie and it landed on the floor, and I felt so cross at the unfairness of everything that I turned to shout at him in a vicious sort of a way, but it came out as a spit.

There was a shocked silence, then Jamie said, "She spat at me!"

"*Ergheuhh* … disgusting!" said Sam.

"Tabitha!" Mum cried. "How *dare* you! Go up to your room."

"It's not fair!" I blazed. "It's really and truly—"

"Go!" Mum said, pointing. "I've been to a funeral and I've had a very tiring day and I don't need to come home here and find all this going on. I really hoped you were learning to control your temper, but…"

Her voice faded as I snatched the cushion, left the kitchen and stamped up the stairs.

I was *furious*. I hated Sam: he was the most loathsome brother anyone had ever had. Not only that, but there were two of them. I not only had a horrible and revolting brother, but I also had one in reserve.

It was while I was stomping across my room

thinking this that the first weird thing happened. It was a bit like when you shiver and say that someone has walked over your grave, and a bit like how a cat might feel if someone had brushed its fur the wrong way. Anyway, I got this strange shuddery feeling all over, just for a moment, and then it went.

I put the cushion on my bed, thinking how nicely it went with the coloured silk sari, and then I found a tape (choosing, of course, a band that everyone else in the house hated), put it in my deck and turned it up as loudly as I dared. This made me feel a lot better.

But I still hated the twins.

CHAPTER FOUR

It was Saturday morning and I was fiddling about in my bedroom. I'd tidied up, re-arranged all my books, and I'd also found some white muslin material in Mum's scrap bag, which I'd twirled round a bamboo stick and placed across the top of my roller blind.

I stood back to look at the exotic effect, quite pleased with it. As I said, I liked my room, but I would have liked it more if it had been bigger. When we'd first come to live in the house I'd been in the bedroom next door, which was twice the size, but once the twins had been born they'd been given it and I'd been pushed out to this one.

I went downstairs, scoffed a bowl of cereal, watched some TV and decided that I'd go over to Emily's house.

I went back upstairs to get dressed and noticed my bedroom door was slightly open.

I was sure I'd shut it, so I was instantly suspicious that *they'd* been in there.

I went in cautiously, pushed the door shut behind me – and the cardboard lid which they'd balanced along the top fell off. As it fell, a mass of tiny pieces of paper, feathers and paperclips showered over the floor, the bed and the worktop.

All over my clean and tidy, near-perfect bedroom! I let out a shriek of rage, flung open the door and hammered on the door of the twins' room. It was locked, of course. Their bedroom, like Mum and Dad's, is big enough to merit having a key. Mine isn't.

"What's going on?" Mum said, coming out of the bathroom. "I did hope we might have a nice quiet weekend." She looked past me and into my bedroom. "Tabitha! Your bedroom looks absolutely disgusting."

"It's them!" I spluttered.

"What d'you mean? The twins? They're playing with their cars. I haven't heard a thing from them all morning." She tutted crossly. "What *have* you been doing – it looks like a jumble sale! Now, I want you to go and get the vacuum cleaner right now and—"

"They did it, Mum!" I cried. "You're not listening to me. You never listen to me!"

Dad appeared up the stairs, sighing heavily. "Do we have to have this first thing in the morning, Tabitha?"

"I didn't start it! It was them!" I said, feeling myself going red.

"Just stop shouting at your mother, Tabitha. That's all I ask."

"I wasn't shouting!" I shouted.

Dad made an impatient gesture, as if he couldn't be bothered to listen. "She's got *such* a temper," Mum said, shaking her head. "I think it's getting worse."

I opened my mouth to protest and then I shut it again. What was the point? What *was* the point? They never listened to me; they always took the twins' side. They were all hateful, all of them.

I went back into my room and slammed the door so hard that the feathers and scraps of paper shifted in the draught. I threw myself down on my bed, fuming, and I heard Mum and Dad go downstairs. For a moment all was quiet, and then I heard a noise from the twins' room, infuriating me beyond measure: the sound of them laughing.

When I heard that I *boiled* with anger. I felt I wanted to tear the wall down, get to them and pick them up and bite them. I wanted to spit and scratch and claw…

And then, quite suddenly, I felt the shivery-shudder that I'd felt a few days before, and then the strangest, weirdest feeling of all: as if I was folding up into myself. As if everything about me was being concentrated into

35

something small, neat and compact.

It happened very quickly. One moment I was sitting on my bed; the next thing I knew, the pattern on my duvet had zoomed in close – I was a lot nearer to it because I'd gone smaller. The other thing I was conscious of was an irritating tickling on my top lip.

I looked down at myself.

I saw black fur.

I saw paws.

And I knew immediately what had happened, just as if I'd halfway known all along. I mean, I didn't think I'd changed into a werewolf or anything, I *knew* what I was.

It wasn't too much of a shock, either, but a bit the way things happen in dreams. You know how the silliest, most incredible, ridiculous things can happen and you don't think anything of them? Well, it was like that. I thought: Oh, I'm a cat.

And when I realized that, I realized what Aunt Mitzi was all about, and why she'd sent me the cushion. And then I realized how significant it had been that I looked like her, and was the only girl in the family to be "one of us". And after that I wondered whether, when she'd come to see me when I was a baby, she'd passed the gift on to me, like the fairies in *Sleeping Beauty* when they come to the christening. And that was a rather nice thought and I didn't feel the slightest bit scared. After all, I

36

thought, if Aunt Mitzi had coped with changing into a cat occasionally, then I could too.

But all these thoughts were skimming through me fast as light, and I hadn't even *seen* myself. I lifted my head and tried to look in the mirror opposite, but of course it was halfway up the wall and I was much too small now.

I jumped down from the bed. As I jumped I thought to myself, *Cats always fall on their feet* – and that's just what I did.

Managing four legs was surprisingly easy, I just thought about moving forwards and everything went into place. I loped across the room smoothly and gracefully, leapt onto my table and peered into my round mirror on its stand.

Yes, I was a cat all right. If I could have done, I would have smiled, because I was quite beautiful. I was sleek and dark and shiny, with glittery green eyes. My ears were shell pink inside, with a downy black fur covering, and where the tickling had been under my nose I'd grown luxuriant, springy whiskers.

I wasn't just any old cat, I was a *gorgeous* cat. I was the cat in Aunt Mitzi's garden.

I admired myself in the mirror for a long time, turning this way and that (nice long tail, bushy in the middle and pointed at the end), and then I walked along the tabletop investigating things. The talc made me sneeze, the shower gel had such a high, sharp scent it made my eyes water, and when I stuck my head in the glass of orange juice standing there, I *hated* it.

I jumped down, landing beautifully, and went under my bed. I put my nose into some fluff and made myself sneeze again, and found a pen I'd been looking for. I also found a ping-pong ball, and I put out a paw and patted it along the carpet. When it rolled away, I pounced on it. Funnily enough, it didn't feel the least bit strange to be under a bed pouncing on a ping-pong ball – just perfectly natural.

I caught the ball, bit it and then lost interest. I sauntered across the carpet, went behind my chest of drawers and discovered a page of homework that I'd lost weeks before. Then I jumped up onto the top of the chest and looked out of the window.

Looking down, I saw Dad getting the car out of the garage and squashed down an urge to yell, "Hey, Dad, look at me!", not knowing how Dad would react if a black cat suddenly called to him from an upstairs window. Besides, I somehow knew that I couldn't speak now, but only miaow.

Dad went inside again and, as my window was wide open (we were having a bit of a heatwave), I stepped through it onto the sill. I walked eight dainty catsteps and came to a small gap. Not even thinking about the possibility of falling, I did a graceful leap onto the twins' windowsill. Their window, like mine, was open and I looked in.

Jamie and Sam were sitting on the floor playing with their cars, pushing them backwards and forwards to each other and rocking with laughter.

"Yeah!"

"Got her, all right!"

"My idea!"

"No, mine!"

My ears twitched as I listened to them. Horrible little *beasts*.

While I was sitting there, half hidden behind their curtain, I suddenly realized that there was a deep growling in the room. I looked further in to see Mutton on red alert, ears cocked, staring towards the window – and me.

I immediately slid back, out of view. As I moved, Mutton gave a yelp, and there was a clatter and a thump as he leapt forward.

He must have barged into the boys' cars, because there was a yell of "Mutton!" and "Stupid dog!"

I stayed well hidden.

"What's up with him?" I heard Sam say, then Jamie said they'd better take him for a walk. A bit after this they went out of their room, locking the door behind them.

They appeared in the front garden with

Mutton. I thought that he, Mutton, might look up, but the soppy thing obviously couldn't make the connection between the windowsill *inside* and the windowsill *outside*, because he didn't.

The three of them disappeared down the road to the park and I slipped into their bedroom.

It was a disgusting mess in there. I had to pick my way through discarded shoes, socks, pants and apple cores – lots of things which smelt foul. I looked round. I wanted to do something, but wasn't sure what. I wanted to do something to get my own back. It was no use just moving things around, though – the state that bedroom was in, no one would notice.

In the end I picked up various things in my teeth: T-shirts, socks, a sweatshirt, a shoe – dragged them to the window and dropped them in a pile onto the concrete outside.

Then I went back to my room and, feeling exhausted, jumped on my bed. The cold cotton duvet didn't feel right underneath me, though. It just wasn't soft and cosy enough. I suddenly spied the red velvet cushion and stepped over to that. I climbed onto it, worked the soft filling beneath my paws until I'd made a little nest for myself, then tucked my head into my tummy, curled my tail around me and gave a deep sigh of contentment which came out as a purr. I closed my eyes and fell asleep.

When I woke up, I was back to being me, Tabitha Brown, a girl, sitting on a cushion.

CHAPTER FIVE

"But *how* could they have?" Sam wailed.

"They couldn't just *jump* out the window…"

I was sitting in the kitchen, quietly reading the paper, when the twins came in, amazed, incredulous and indignant about the pile of stuff they'd found tossed into the front garden.

"How could anyone have got in our bedroom?" Jamie said.

"The door was locked!" said Sam. He eyed Jamie's things suspiciously. "There were more of mine thrown out."

"No, there weren't," Jamie said promptly. "There were more of *mine*."

"Well, I'm sorry they fell out, but you shouldn't leave them on the windowsill," Mum said.

"We didn't!"

"They were on the floor!"

"Now, boys," Mum said, "talk sense. They couldn't have been on the floor. They didn't *fly* out of the window." She appealed to me. "They couldn't have been on the floor, could they, Tabitha?"

"No, of course not," I said reasonably.

"Quite," Mum said. "You must have been clearing up and put a pile of stuff on the windowsill and forgotten about it."

I nodded. "Then a freak wind must have blown everything out." I smirked to myself as I spoke: the freak wind idea sounded ridiculous. But not quite as ridiculous as saying that I'd changed into a cat, picked the things up in my teeth and dropped them out. "They *had* to be on the windowsill," I said.

"They weren't!"

"They were on the floor!"

"There were more of my things!"

"More of mine!"

"Perhaps a mysterious dark force picked them up and whirled them out," I suggested. I spoke softly so that Mum couldn't hear; she didn't hold with such things. "Like in *The X-Files*."

Jamie gave a scream.

"Mysterious dark force! Wow!" Sam said, and they looked at each other in alarm.

"So, I should be very careful what you do from now on – watch out for strange happenings," I said, thinking to myself that there was

43

one good thing about having twin brothers: when you got revenge you got it twice.

"And now could you take all this stuff upstairs and put it away, boys," Mum said briskly, turning with a saucepan of soup. "And all I can say is you must take better care from now on."

"It's not fair!" Jamie said.

"My T-shirt went in a puddle," said Sam.

Mutton pushed through the half-open kitchen door, covered in foam because Dad was washing the car. Mutton was soppy at the best of times, but at weekends he turned into a sort of brainless, bouncing mass, joining in everything that was going on, chasing anything that moved and eating anything that didn't.

Sam, scowling deeply, patted his side. "Here, boy!" he said to Mutton.

Mutton began shaking himself, sending flecks of foam everywhere. Suddenly, though, he went very still, very rigid. His hackles rose. He was facing the other way, but when he went rigid he looked over his shoulder and stared at me. His lips went back, showing his teeth.

"Hey, look at Mutton!" Jamie said.

"His wild's up!"

"No, no. He's scared of something," Mum said. She looked at me. "Have you been shouting at him, Tabitha?"

"'Course I haven't," I gulped. To tell you

44

the truth, I was as taken aback as she was. It was as if the soppy dog knew something. "How could you scare *him*? He's too daft to be scared of anything. Boo!" I said half-heartedly.

Mutton went into the furthest corner of the kitchen, behind the waste bin, and cowered there, looking at me with wide eyes.

"Come here, boy!" Jamie said. "What's she been doing to you?"

But Mutton wouldn't come out – not until he was dragged, and then he slunk round the edge of the room, not taking his eyes off me.

I can't say I minded. As I think I've mentioned, I've never really liked him; he's too slobbery-wet around the mouth and (on the occasions when I've been forced to take him for a walk) too keen on sniffing other dogs' bottoms for my liking. I'd never actually be nasty to him – but for him to stay at arm's length suited me just fine. In fact, it would be a positive pleasure not being bounced at, licked and sniffed every time I came into a room.

It was funny, that, I thought as I went upstairs, I'd never really liked dogs, and now there was a reason why.

I sat on my bed, wondering about things – like, how often was the changing going to happen? And what was I going to do if it happened at school, or while I was with someone?

Would I always know long enough in advance to be able to run into the loo and hide?

Another thing: was I going to tell anyone? Should I tell Mum? Should I tell Emily? What would happen if I did – would the power go away?

And suppose I decided I really didn't like it happening? Could I get out of it? Pass it on to someone else? *What were the rules?*

Thinking about it, I decided I probably wouldn't want to pass it to someone else – not yet, at any rate. It seemed to be the sort of thing that you accepted, like being born a girl. It had its drawbacks but you just got on with it and enjoyed the best bits. And I wouldn't tell anyone else, either. Apart from the fact that (a) they wouldn't believe me and (b) they'd think I'd gone potty, once people knew, I wouldn't be able to play tricks. And I did quite fancy getting my own back on the twins a few dozen times...

I got a black sweatshirt out of my cupboard to wear to Emily's, thinking that another funny thing was that I'd always liked wearing black, even when I was quite little. This led me to wonder whether, if I'd changed into a tabby cat, I'd have liked tabby brown-coloured clothes. Or if I was a Siamese, cream with coffee-coloured accessories, perhaps?

An hour later I was at Emily's, watching her

do her ballet exercises. She was practising at the barre, counting in French in a rather showing-off way all the while: *un-deux-trois-quatre-cinq* and so on.

I yawned. "How long are you going to practise? Aren't we going to walk into town? Salamanders has got a sale on."

"What d'you want to buy there? *Un-deux-trois; un-deux-trois…*"

"It's got Indian print rugs. I want to see how much they are. I want my bedroom more exotic."

"*And* plié *and rest…*" She sat down on the bed. "It's exotic already. And you could hardly fit anything else in."

"I know. It's pathetically small. Too small to …" I grinned to myself, "swing a cat."

She stood up again and began bending from the waist, sweeping her hands onto the floor. "I wish you'd take up ballet," she said, "then we could practise together and go to London to see shows."

I screwed up my face. "I'm no good at learning routines. And I've never much fancied it, anyway."

"No, I suppose it's not really you, is it?" Emily said, and added smugly, "We can't *all* have talent."

I looked at her, niggled. "We might not all be able to hold onto a long bit of wood and bend over double, but some of us might be able to do other things. *I* might have a talent that you don't know about."

"If everyone had a talent," Emily mused, "then they'd all be on stage being talented and there wouldn't be anyone – anyone ordinary – left to be an audience."

"I might *not* be ordinary. I might be able to do something quite amazing."

"That would be really funny, wouldn't it? I mean, suppose everyone was really good at something."

"Something really ... quite ... extraordinary..."

"They'd be so busy doing that, no one would ever go to see anyone else." She frowned at me. "What d'you mean? What can you do that's so clever?"

I paused. "I didn't say I *could* do anything, just that I might be able to..."

"Oh, I see! Because I was going to say, if you *have* got a talent you've been keeping it pretty quiet."

That did it. I hesitated for a moment, then thought to myself that it sounded so ridiculous she probably wouldn't believe me anyway. Besides, nothing exciting had ever happened to me before, and it seemed a pity not to make full use of it.

"I can turn into a cat," I said.

"Oh? So can I." She made her hands into paws and tried to look cute. "*Miaow. Miaow.*"

"Not like that. Really."

"What d'you mean, really? Put on a cat costume, you mean? Anyone can do that."

"No. *Really*. Like magic or something." I lowered my voice. "I really *can* turn into a cat."

"Go on, then," she said. "Do it now."

"I can't just do—"

"Oh, there's a surprise!"

"No. It happens – well, I think this is how it works. When I'm angry, when I lose my temper—"

"Well, get angry then." She threw a cushion at me. "You're a greedy pig and I hate you. Is that enough?"

I shook my head. "It's not like that." I frowned. "It's only happened once so far."

"What – once in your life?"

I nodded. "It's only just come – this talent or ability or whatever you call it. It came from Aunt Mitzi."

"What d'you mean? How did it come?" she challenged.

"On a cushion."

She burst out laughing.

"Or *with* a cushion, but that was just the sort of emblem. It was handed down, I suppose. Inherited. She used to change into a cat, you see. But I didn't know it until now."

"Oh yeah!" said Emily. "*Very* likely, that is." She paused. "You know my mum's

49

budgie? Well, he's really my Auntie Ruth!"

"Don't believe me, then," I said.

She giggled. "Just because I'm amazingly good at ballet, you don't have to make up something like that."

"OK then," I said. "When it happens again, I'll come round." I thought for a moment. "*If* it happens again. It might not."

She grinned. "No, it might not. What a surprise that would be."

CHAPTER SIX

A few days later, Emily came round to my house.

"Hello! Changed into a cat lately?" she said as she came in my room.

"Sssh…" I said.

She closed the door behind her. "Well, have you?"

"No, I haven't," I said.

"Oh dear," she said sarcastically. "D'you think perhaps you might have lost the power?"

"Don't know," I said, shrugging. When it – the changing – had happened, it had been when I was ragingly angry, but I hadn't been in a bad temper since then. I'd *tried* to get into one: two nights ago I'd watched something on TV about the testing of shampoos on animals and I'd been really furious. Ah ha! I'd thought, and holding onto the furiousness I'd run upstairs, clenched my teeth, held my breath and tried desperately to *force* myself to change, but it hadn't worked.

"Perhaps you'd better take up ballet after all," Emily said, flopping down on my bed and managing to pull one edge of the canopy crooked.

I kept a dignified silence. She'd find out. All in good time.

"What sort of cat are you, anyway?" she went on. "I suppose you're a pedigree. Are you the sort that wins prizes at cat shows?"

"I don't know," I said irritably. I was beginning to wish I'd never told her.

"Are you a posh cat? Persian or something?"

"If you must know, I'm a black cat," I muttered.

"Oh yeah, I s'pose you would be," she said. "Black cat, black magic and all that. Witches' cats are black, aren't they?"

"I didn't decide to be black," I said. "That's just what I turned out to be."

"Here – we've got two black cats living down the road at number thirty-six. If you come round when you're a cat, how will I know it's you?"

"Don't worry, I'll sit outside your window and miaow," I said bitterly.

"*They* do that. Can't you just speak and tell me who you are?"

"No, I can't," I said shortly. "I'm not a performing cat."

"I just thought—"

"And I'm not a girl *pretending* to be a cat, either. When it happens, I *am* a cat."

Emily pulled a face. "Get you. It's only a joke, isn't it? No need to get ratty." She grinned and added, "Or catty."

"Oh, very good," I said, and things were a bit strained between us for the rest of the afternoon.

I knew how she felt, though. I mean, if *she'd* told *me* that she could change into a cat I'd never have believed her. Not in a hundred years. I'd have to see proof first. I'd have to see her, as a cat, right in front of my eyes, and then she'd have to do something to prove that it was her under the fur. And even then I don't know if I'd have believed it.

The next day I was going past Mrs Neil-next-door's house when she called me over and asked me if I had anything to do for the summer holidays.

"I've got some project work for school," I said. "Is that what you mean?"

"Well, it's like this," she said. "I was wondering if you'd like a little job so you could earn a few pounds for yourself."

"Mum wouldn't let me," I said.

"But she'd let you do a few things for me

around the garden, wouldn't she?"

I nodded fairly eagerly. There were things I wanted to buy: bits for my bedroom, of course, and clothes – and I always wanted more cassettes, the more hip-hoppier the better to annoy the twins. "What d'you want done?"

"It's the front garden," she said. "It's a terrible mess. If you could weed it first and dig it over, I'd give you a couple of trays of bedding plants to put in. It shouldn't take you more than an hour, and if you get on all right you could do it regularly for me."

"OK," I said. I wanted to ask how much, but I didn't know how to say it without its sounding rude. Later, I really wished I had done.

I didn't go home and ask Mum, because she was out with the twins – they'd gone to the zoo. I'd been asked along too, of course, and in view of what had happened I quite fancied seeing the big cats, but I don't like zoos and I especially don't like zoos which have Jamie and Sam in them, so I'd turned the offer down. I started on the garden straight away.

I really worked hard, considering I'm not keen on things like gardening and I hate getting my hands dirty, and also considering Mrs Neil-next-door kept breathing down my neck the whole time, saying, "Missed a bit there!" or, whenever I pulled up something that I shouldn't have done, "Oh, heavens! You've got no idea, have you!" and tutting a lot.

When she wasn't following me and commenting, she was sitting on a garden chair by her front door, with her dress pulled right up showing her fat legs to anyone who cared to look.

Two and a half hours later, when I'd finished weeding, she came out with four trays of little green plants and a round thingy that made the holes for them to go in. And *then* I had to water everything, and after I'd watered she went round feeling the earth and saying that she wasn't sure if it was watered enough or if the plants were in firmly enough or in straight enough lines.

The whole job took nearly four hours, and she didn't even give me a drink halfway through. I kept at it, though, working out all the time what I was going to spend the money on and wondering what my hourly rate would be, but when I said that I'd finished, d'you know what she held out to me? Two pounds! Two measly pounds.

"There you are. I'm giving you this in spite of all the mistakes," she said. "I just hope you're not going to take up horticulture as a career!"

I stared at her, so angry that I couldn't trust myself to speak.

"And you'll come back later and give them

another water, will you?" she added.

I opened my mouth, about to say something that Mum was certainly going to tell me off for later, but before I could speak I felt the shivery-shuddery feeling again and could do no more than grab the money off her and run.

I heard her say, "There's no need to snatch!" as I tore down her path, went up our own and round the back of the house.

Our shed door was open. I ran through and pushed it shut behind me – just a moment before I realized that I shouldn't have done, because if what I thought was happening actually *was* happening, then there was no way I was going to be able to turn the handle and get out.

And then it was too late to worry about the finer details, because I was a cat again.

I breathed in deeply, staring down at my paws and at the two pound coins on the floor between them, and then I shook my head and twirled my tail, feeling my fur quivering gently all over. There wasn't a mirror in the shed, but I didn't need one. I *knew* I was beautiful.

My paws were filthy, though. I lifted the front right one and began to wash it, licking it with my rough tongue and lightly gnawing the pads with my teeth. When I'd finished and they were nicely pink, I did a quick once-over of my face.

There seemed to be no rush; I felt quite at

peace and as if I had all the time in the world.

I carefully did my ears, inside and out, then carried on licking right down my front. I sat around for a while, sniffing a strange mustiness that I thought might be a mouse, and then I got a bit bored. I was ready to go.

I couldn't open the shed door, of course, but I sprang onto the work bench and, by stretching upwards and pulling myself onto a small, narrow shelf, managed to slip out of the window.

Mutton was tied up on a long rope asleep under a tree and I was tempted to wake him and taunt him, but I had something far more interesting to do. I went into the front and leapt gracefully over the wall into Mrs Neil-next-door's garden.

She'd gone inside, leaving the remains of a tray of tea and a plate with one biscuit on it by her chair. Ignoring this, I trotted over to the flower beds.

Coming to the first seedling I'd planted, I raked my claws over the surface of the ground until it came out. I pulled out three more, then for an interesting variation turned, scrabbled my back paws and got four out at the same time, kicking lots of dirt into the air as I did so. After that I systematically went down the flower bed, kicking and scratching until every last seedling was up and lying on the top.

Good work! I admired the scene, and was

just going to trot off when I glanced again at the freshly dug earth and was terribly tempted. It looked *so* inviting that I just had to go and have a little sprinkle, right in the middle of it.

After that I modestly covered my tracks, then went back to her tea tray and stuck my head inside the jug to drink some of the milk. Following all this excitement I went into my own garden to sit on the front wall and watch the world go by.

This was fun. I had no worries, no responsibilities, I just had to sit there and be admired.

The woman from three doors down came by.

"Nice puss!" she said, and she put out her hand towards me. I felt a bit nervous at first – she was a big woman and with one smack she could have knocked me off the wall, but she just tickled me on the nose with her finger and then scratched right round my ears. It felt wonderful; it felt so good that I found myself purring.

I loved being out there, sitting in the sun and having people stroke me and say, "You're a lovely cat!" or "There's a nice pussy!" or whatever. I found that if I looked directly at people, they seldom passed without giving me a pat. Some even said things to me that required a reply, like, "Enjoying the sun?" or "Not too hot for you, is it?"

I was hoping Mrs Neil-next-door would

come out and discover her plants while I was there, but unfortunately she didn't.

What did happen, though, was that after about ten minutes Mum and the twins drove up. The boys totally ignored me, racing through the gate and round the back to Mutton, but Mum looked at me and paused.

"Hello, puss. You're a fine boy, aren't you?" she said, and then tickled under my chin. I purred, pushing my nose up into her hand.

"Who do *you* belong to?" Mum said.

I gave a little miaow. My first, I believe.

Mum laughed. "There's a clever cat. I think you're trying to tell me!"

The twins came round the house with Mutton on his long rope. Jamie tripped Sam up with it and they both started yelling.

"Oh dear. We're home," Mum said, and she gave me one last tickle and began to walk up the path to the front door.

Sam picked himself up and saw me. "There's a cat! Go, boy!" he urged Mutton.

"Get it!" Jamie yelled.

"You leave that cat alone," Mum said.

Mutton began racing down the path towards me and then – well, you know how cartoon characters stop? – he suddenly came to a shuddering halt.

I sat there, calmly looking at him. My only movement was in my tail, which was swishing slowly from side to side. It said: *Just you dare…*

"Go on, boy!" Jamie urged. "See it off!"

But Mutton was looking at me as if I was a full-sized tiger. He took the widest possible path around me, going miles out on his rope.

Jamie's mouth fell open in surprise. "What's he doing that for?"

"Why's he scared of a cat?!" said Sam.

"He's spooked," I wanted to say, but unfortunately I couldn't.

This didn't stop me thinking that I'd struck a decent blow for cats' liberation, and that Aunt Mitzi would have been proud.

CHAPTER SEVEN

I waited until Mutton and the boys had gone tearing down the road, and then I jumped off the wall and began to make my way along the pavement towards Emily's house. Here was a chance to show off the new pussy me in all my glory. I didn't feel as if I was about to change back, and anyway, I'd had an idea about this – about changing – which I was going to try out later.

The pavements and walls beneath my paws were dry and warm and I enjoyed walking along them, tail held high, receiving more admiring glances. Well, not quite everyone admired me. Some people's eyes just went straight over me, and one or two even seemed to look at me as if I was something rather disagreeable. It made me think about what Aunt Mitzi had said – about people being either cat or dog people.

I didn't meet any actual dogs, which was a pity, because I wanted to see if all of them, not just Mutton, were scared of me. I came across a cat, though, a big ginger one, name of Marmalade, who lived at number eighty at the end of our road. I was trotting along his low, brick, garden wall when I saw him fast asleep under a bush right next to me.

I stopped and stared down at him, taking in all sorts of fascinating things I'd never noticed before: the way his ears were quite white inside, and the fact that, unlike me, he had hardly any top whiskers above his eyes. On the other hand – or paw, if you like – he had a very nice, bushy tail, with clearly defined orange and brown stripes right down its length. Another thing: I just knew Marmalade *was* a he, in the way you immediately know whether a person you're looking at is a boy or a girl, even if they're wearing jeans and a T-shirt and have cropped hair.

While I was peering down and delicately sniffing the air around him to find out what he'd been up to lately, he lifted his head and saw me.

He scrambled to his feet and gave a long, low growl and a hiss, and his eyes went all slitty and wicked.

I didn't feel particularly cross with *him*, but I felt that some sort of response was called for, so I lowered my body and gave a hiss in return, making the fur rise all along my back. That felt nice and tingly and shivery, so I did it again.

I stood my ground and Marmalade began retreating. I didn't know whether this was because he was a scaredy-cat or if he could sense that there was something odd and not altogether *cat* about me, but anyhow he went backwards across his lawn, and then he turned tail and whipped around the corner.

My fur went down, and I sat for a moment to recover myself before carrying on walking. Emily lived just a couple of streets away, and it only took a few more minutes to get there.

Reaching her house I was pleased to see that her bike was outside, which meant she was in. I went over the fence and round the back to their sitting-room and jumped up on the windowsill. Emily was lying on the floor watching one of the soaps and her mum was sitting on the sofa next to her. Seeing her mum there threw me at first, but then I realized that if she saw me she'd only see a black cat, I didn't have a sign round my neck saying who I was. I wasn't sure if I'd get a warm welcome, though, because I seemed to remember her mum didn't much like cats. She had a bit of a thing about cleanliness and tidiness, and held daily bedroom inspections.

I couldn't tap on the window to Emily, but I stretched up with my paws and dragged them down the glass to make a squeaky noise.

Neither Emily nor her mum turned. I did it again, but they had their backs to me and the TV was quite loud so they obviously couldn't hear.

I looked around. There was a top window open but I could hardly just jump through; her mum would think that was really odd.

Stuck for what to do next, I paced up and down. Here was I, all changed into a cat and ready to prove it, and Emily wasn't even looking. I tried out a couple of *miaows*, but no one heard them, either.

I was resigning myself to sitting there for as long as it took, and wondering what would happen if I changed back unexpectedly – what would Emily and her mum say if they turned to see me, Tabitha, crouched on their windowsill? – when the soap ended. Emily jumped up and went out of the room. Through the doorway I glimpsed her going upstairs, so I went round to the front, to where her bedroom was.

I stared up at her room, where I could now hear one of her ballet cassettes – *The Sleeping Beauty* or something – being played, but I couldn't see a way to get in. There were no trees nearby or flat roofs or garages to give me a way up. I eyed the drainpipes, but I wasn't sure if I had the necessary climbing skills.

I washed round my ears for a while, then stalked to the back again, trying to think of something I could do to prove to Emily that I'd been there. Prowling round the garden, I suddenly caught an intoxicating whiff of mouse. It was like sniffing your favourite meal when you're starving – and more. It was quite irresistible.

I followed the whiff to the back of the shed in Emily's garden, and then I crouched behind a bush and waited.

After a few minutes, I heard a scrabbling noise and two mice came from under the shed, one behind the other.

My heart leapt and, inside, I gave the cat equivalent of a gasp of excitement. My whiskers quivered, I held my breath, my whole body flattened to the ground and was steady.

I watched as the first mouse disappeared through a crack in the back fence. The second was about to follow. I felt myself tense, gather all my strength into my legs, and leap on it just before it disappeared.

I caught it! Caught it between my front paws! And before I could think about what I was doing I'd bitten it at the back of its neck and it was still.

And even then the fun didn't stop. I threw it up into the air, caught it, held it in my teeth and shook it. I volleyballed it from the top of the garden to the bottom. I played cat and mouse good and proper.

It took me about fifteen minutes to get tired of it. And then I took it in my teeth, jumped up on the back windowsill and left it as a little present for Emily.

The journey back was uneventful, with no sign of Marmalade, but when I got home I found that both the front and back doors were closed. Carefully (there were lots of nice lumpy bits on the branches to cling onto) I climbed up the tree that stood next to the twins' bedroom and was about to leap across from their windowsill to my own, when I decided to make a slight detour. I'd look in on them, I decided. I had a bit of a scheme hatching in my head...

I peered through their window. Mutton was asleep in his basket, Jamie was watching TV on the little portable and Sam was playing with cars on a great big plastic roadway that Dad had made for them.

He was pushing a car from one end of the track to the other, and I found this quite fascinating to watch. My head went from side to side, backwards and forwards, following the car intently. It was like the mouse all over again; I was absolutely dying to rush in and leap on it.

The car suddenly went off the track and, remembering what I was there for, I made sure I was hidden, then made a high, wild and wailing noise, a proper "cat on the tiles" cry.

It worked a treat. Mutton began a bark of panic, and I glimpsed Jamie and Sam looking at each other, alarmed.

"Whassat?" I heard Jamie asking.

Quick as a flash I went along the window-sill, through my own window and onto the cushion. I twirled round on it a few times to get comfortable, then while I was twirling I had an idea. I jumped up and went over to a T-shirt I'd left on the bed. I made myself comfortable on this (I liked the smell; it smelled of *me*), put my head between my paws and closed my eyes.

I heard the twins thundering downstairs and then, almost immediately, it seemed, I was me again, lying on my bed on a T-shirt.

I stood up and stretched. It was as I'd thought: it seemed that I only had to go to sleep to change back. I didn't even have to go to sleep *on the cushion*. So that meant, probably, that I could troll around happily as a cat for as long as I liked – or as long as I could safely be missing – without fear of changing back in the middle of the street.

I went downstairs and into the sitting-room, where Mum was sitting with her feet up having a cup of tea. The twins were banging on about "an awful wailing noise" and "a horrible blood-curdling scream" and Mum was telling them not to be so silly, and that it must just have been someone in the street who'd cried out.

She asked me where I'd been and I said,

quite truthfully, to Emily's. I also said that I'd left something at her house and wanted to ring her, and then I went into the kitchen for a couple of biscuits and took the telephone into the cupboard under the stairs so I wouldn't be interrupted.

"It's me," I said when Emily answered. "I've just been round."

"What d'you mean you've been round?" she asked. "Why didn't you knock, then?"

"Couldn't. Didn't have hands," I said.

"What are you going on about?"

"Well, paws aren't quite as flexible."

"You're not talking about that cat business again, are you?"

"You asked me to come round when I changed," I said, "and I just changed, so I did."

"Oh, right," she said heavily. "Let's get this straight: you're asking me to believe that you changed into a black cat, then came round and miaowed outside my house, are you?"

"That's right," I said. "I went round the back and you were watching the soap before the news, and your mum was with you, then you went upstairs and put on one of your ballets. *The Sleeping Beauty*."

There was a moment's silence and I knew she was frowning. "Good guess," she said after a moment, "but not enough. You know I always watch that soap and I'm always

68

practising to ballet cassettes. And it was *Coppélia* anyway."

"OK, then," I said. "Go outside your sitting-room window and look on the windowsill."

"Now?"

"Right now. There's a present there for you," I added tantalizingly.

She was away for a moment or two, during which time the twins made their way upstairs still going on about the wailing they'd heard, only now they were saying it was like a pack of werewolves.

"*Yuck!*" said Emily when she came back on.

"Was it still there?" I asked eagerly.

"That dead mouse? Yes, it was. Oh, Tabitha, how could you?"

"Well, first I stalked it, then I pounced and then I bit—"

"Don't!" she said. "The poor little thing."

"Don't be daft," I said, "it's only a mouse!"

"Only a mouse! I thought you liked animals."

"I do, but—"

"I can't believe you actually ... did you find it dead in the garden?"

"No, I killed it myself, I told you."

"Killed it yourself! I can't believe it. Are you going to kill other things? Are you going to work up to cats and dogs? God, before you know where you are you'll be killing cows and horses!"

"Don't be daft, of course I won't! I just…" I thought back to how it had happened. "I just sort of did it on impulse. I couldn't help myself."

"A dear little mouse!"

"I didn't think of it as a dear little mouse," I faltered. Suddenly I saw the mouse as a tiny, furry, cute thing, not as prey.

"Even if you did find it dead, to pick it up and put it on the windowsill! I mean, I can't bear to *touch* it. I'm going to get a shovel and dig a nice hole in the garden and bury it properly. In a white cardboard box," she added.

There was a long silence.

"All right, well – sorry," I said awkwardly. "I only put it there so you'd know I'd been a cat when I came round."

"I don't know anything of the sort," she said sniffily. "You could quite easily have crept into the garden and put it there as a person. Though how you—"

"Well, I didn't," I interrupted, but thought it best not to mention the killing again. I had to admit, actually, that it did now sound a bit bloodthirsty, especially for someone who (when a girl) was trying to be a vegetarian.

"Are you still a cat at the moment?" Emily asked.

"Of course I'm not. How could I dial your number with paws? Besides, I wouldn't be able to speak."

"Oh no. I forgot."

I sighed. "Look, let's leave it," I said. "I'll see you tomorrow – we're supposed to be going to the library to start the project. The Victorian servant one."

"All right. And we won't talk about the cat business, OK?"

"OK," I said resignedly. She was never going to believe me. Never. Not unless I went round there as a cat and paraded in front of her. And even then I'd probably have to miaow our school song while walking on my back legs.

CHAPTER EIGHT

"No!" I said to Mrs Neil-next-door in pretend amazement. It was quite early – I was still in my pyjamas – and she was on the doorstep describing the shock-horror that had hit her that morning when she'd seen the garden. "After *all* that work I did!" I said pointedly.

"I couldn't believe it," she blustered, "just couldn't believe it! I went out last thing at night to give them a bit of a drink, because I wasn't at all sure you'd watered them in enough, and they were all up and lying on the top of the ground. Every last one of them."

"What's that?" Mum said behind me. "Do ask Mrs Neil in, Tabitha. Don't leave her standing on the step."

Mrs Neil-next-door didn't need asking twice. She came through the front door and into the kitchen, bristling with indignation.

"Mum, you know I did *all* that work in Mrs

Neil's garden yesterday," I said. (I'd told her, naturally, about the huge amount of work for the small amount of payment.) "Well, a cat dug up all the plants!"

Mrs Neil-next-door looked at me hard. "I didn't say it was a cat," she said. "I said a *scavenger*."

Ooops, I thought. I'd fallen into the trap that murderers fall into when cross-examined by a detective. *("But I didn't say that he was stabbed, I merely said he was dead.")*

"Oh, I thought you did," I said.

"As a matter of fact, I thought it might be a dog."

I saw then why she'd come round: to hint strongly that it was Mutton, so that one of us would feel obliged to put things right.

"Oh, it wouldn't be our dog," Mum said immediately, holding up the teapot towards Mrs Neil-next-door as an invitation. "Not our Mutton."

Mrs Neil-next-door nodded *yes* to the teapot. "Of course not," she said. "I know your Mutton wouldn't do a thing like that. No, some other dog. Some stray."

"I haven't seen any strays around here lately," Mum said, shaking her head. "And it's more likely to be a cat, I should think."

"Well, the whole thing is shocking," Mrs Neil-next-door went on. "After so much work, too." She looked at me. "Perhaps you'd be able to give me a few minutes later today, Tabitha. If you work quickly you'll be able to replant everything in half an hour."

I shook my head. "Sorry," I said, trying to sound regretful.

Mum poured out the tea. "Can't you even manage a short time, Tabitha?"

"No," I said. "I've arranged to go to the library with Emily. We're working on our school project." As I spoke I adopted an earnest and hardworking expression, knowing full well that Mum would never ask me to do anything which interfered with the sanctity of a *school project*.

"It's disgusting that people don't keep pets under control," said Mrs Neil-next-door. "They let them run around other people's gardens willy-nilly, *ruining* their planting."

Mum sat down with her tea, looking thoughtful. "I did see a strange black cat around here yesterday," she said. "It was sitting on our front wall when I came home."

"Perhaps it was him, then," Mrs Neil-next-door said. "Nasty sly creatures, cats."

"Oh, d'you think so?" I said. "I like them." I turned to Mum and couldn't resist asking, "Was it a nice cat?"

"It was a beautiful cat," Mum said. "Very sleek and glossy. Like the ones you see sitting in tulips on greetings cards."

"So you wouldn't be able to give me even a

few minutes…" Mrs Neil-next-door wheedled.

"Sorry!" I said cheerfully, getting up from the table. "Big project on. Better get dressed – I've got to get to the library."

When I came out of the bathroom I passed the twins' room. They were going full throttle and sounding like a cartoon – *Ooof! Yaahh! Boof! Whuff!* – and I decided they were probably having a pillow-fight.

I knew Mutton was in the garden, so I wouldn't be able to wind him up, but I couldn't resist running my nails lightly over the twins' door and making a faint scratching sound. I also did a faraway *Whooo!* noise.

They heard that all right.

"Whassat?" I heard Jamie ask, and they went quiet.

I did one more scratch and one more *Whooo!* for effect, then disappeared quietly into my own room and picked up a book.

They were out of their room and in mine within seconds.

"Did you hear something?" Jamie asked.

"Like what?"

"A funny noise," he said fearfully.

"A scratching and a moaning!" Sam said.

"I didn't hear a thing!"

"D'you really think this house is haunted?" Jamie asked.

"Could be," I said, and just to guard against

them going and telling Mum I'd said so, added, "but I don't suppose so. You've probably been watching too many *X-Files*."

"Bet it is haunted!" Sam said.

"We're going to get Scully and Mulder to investigate."

"They're made-up people," I said. "They're just actors playing a part. They're not real."

"Well, someone like them," Jamie went on, "because this house is definitely haunted."

"Funny things happen," Sam said, looking anxious. "And we keep hearing things."

"Well, I don't," I said. "So perhaps it's not the *house* that's haunted."

"What d'you mean?"

"Perhaps it's just your room," I said lightly, and I returned to my book.

There, I thought. That would put the cat among the pigeons.

Later, at the library with Emily, when we'd written pages and pages about Victorian servants and were fed up with them, she moved along the rows and started looking at the ballet books and I picked out a few books on cats. We were in the children's reference section, so these weren't terribly interesting: mostly of the "Here's a pretty little pussy in a basket" variety, advising you to get your cat's flu inoculations boosted each year and to worm it regularly.

I wriggled uncomfortably on my seat. *Worms*. I hoped my times as a cat were going to be short and I wouldn't have to worry. I also hoped that I wasn't going to be a cat long enough to get hungry, because I didn't fancy eating tinned cat food in the slightest, especially if it was in jelly.

I studied the photographs of the kittens in the book. They were playing with knitting, having pink bows tied round their necks or playing with balls – and they were all dead cute. Suppose, I suddenly thought, that some of *them* were sometimes people. They might be. Or was I actually the only girl in the entire world who was able to turn into a cat?

This led me to have another thought and I went over to where Emily was sitting.

"Look at this!" she said, showing me a photo of two people standing on their toes. "Nureyev and Fonteyn in *La Fille mal Gardée*. Don't they look absolutely wonderful?"

I nodded. "Very nice," I said. "Look. About me being a ... turning into a cat."

She looked up. "I thought we weren't going to talk about it."

"I just want to say something," I said. "I know you don't believe me."

"No."

"And I'm not saying anything about that now, or trying to persuade you, I just want to ask you something."

"What?"

I cleared my throat. "If you ever *do* believe me, you won't tell anyone, will you?"

"'Course not," she said. "Everyone would think I was mad."

"Apart from that," I said earnestly, "I was thinking about ET."

"Don't tell me – now you're an extra-terrestrial."

"Don't be ridiculous," I said. "I was just thinking about the bit in the film where they track him down and take him off to be investigated, and how awful it was. If they find out about me changing into a cat I'd be taken away, wouldn't I? And I don't want to be locked up in some scientific place and studied."

"No, I suppose not." She smirked. "It would be a bit of a *cat*astrophe, wouldn't it?"

I looked at her witheringly.

"OK," she said, shrugging. "I promise not to tell."

"Not ever?"

"Not ever," she said.

"On … Margot Fonteyn's life?"

"She's dead."

"Oh well. Someone's life," I said.

"I won't *ever* tell," she said solemnly. "If you turn up on my doorstep as a black cat, I'll just give you a saucer of milk, tickle you under your chin and send you on your way."

CHAPTER NINE

I stretched out deliciously, right from the pale pink pads of my paws to the slim, sleek point of my tail. I felt taut and tingly all over when I did this, and as if I'd doubled in length.

After I'd stretched I lay on my bedroom carpet for a moment, completely relaxed, then I tucked my paws under me, curled my tail around snugly and began to purr. I *liked* this feeling; I liked changing. It all went so smoothly and naturally: one minute I'd be furious, hateful and gnarled up – and then I'd change and feel all unruffled and self-satisfied, singing a purry song of contentment.

It had been Dad who'd set me off changing this morning. Dad and *them*, of course. It was Saturday and, because Jamie and Sam had been going on for ages about wanting new trainers, Dad had said he'd take them into town to buy them. I needed new trainers, too, actually, but the two of them together make more fuss than one of me, so they were getting taken out to buy theirs and I wasn't.

Anyway, Dad went out to the garden shed to clean his shoes ready to go out, and he came back into the kitchen with two pound coins, which he put on the table.

"What do you think?" he said to me and the twins. "I found them on the floor of the shed. Who do you think they belong to?"

I was eating a piece of toast at the time, and I nearly choked on it. I'd forgotten to go in the shed and pick up the two pounds that I'd got for the drudgery in the garden! It wasn't like me to forget about money, especially when it was hard-earned, but then changing into a cat does rather drive other, smaller, things out of your head.

"It's mine!" I said, at the same time as Sam yelled, "Mine!"

We glowered at each other and of course there was some hassle about it and a bit of shouting, and Dad took Sam's side, and I ended up being so angry that I shoved my plate across the table and half a slice of toast went with it and slid onto the floor. When this happened Dad shouted at me, then I ran out of the kitchen and up the stairs to my room and *transmogrified*.

This is a real word, by the way, which I heard on TV two nights ago. When I looked it up I found that it meant to transform yourself in a *surprising or magical manner*. Which is me, isn't it? And best of all, it's got *mog* in the middle, so I think it's a special and appropriate word for changing into a cat.

After I'd stretched right across my carpet I yawned once or twice, slowly and lazily, then rolled across the floor and rubbed my head on the leg of the bed. While I was doing this I heard Dad and the twins go out. They all shouted up goodbye, and Sam also called, "Temper, temper!" which usually makes me absolutely furious, but which in my present state just made me want to purr harder. I jumped up on my windowsill and watched them go down the road.

They disappeared but I just stayed there, blinking happily in the sunlight, wondering what to do next. I had to go and see Emily, that was a must, but as Mum had gone to the Saturday market and I had the house to myself, it seemed a shame not to do anything cattish about the place. And something which would slightly spook the twins, of course, and move on my plan.

I walked along the windowsill to their bedroom, went in through the window and looked round. What could I do? What would unnerve them?

I twitched my whiskers as I walked round looking at things and thinking. After a while,

I decided to get together all the toy cars I could find. I found about fifty, and I either picked them up in my mouth or tapped them gently with my paw, arranging them into an X. This, I thought, could either mean X the unknown, or *X-Files*. When I'd done this I climbed back out of the window and into the tree, and after some thought went down backwards, holding on by digging my claws into the bark.

At the bottom I paused and watched a small flock of birds scatter on sight of me, then went round to the back of our house and squeezed through the small window above the sink, which had been left slightly open. Jumping onto the sink unit and cleverly avoiding a puddle of water, I leapt from here onto the kitchen table.

In the middle were the two pound coins and a note to Mum which read:

Gone into town to get the trainers. Is this your money? Found it in the shed and it caused a riot, so have confiscated it from all. See you later x x x

I was just thinking about chewing up the note and hiding the coins away somewhere I could collect them later, when I heard Mum coming in. I immediately jumped down from the kitchen table and, assuming a docile, good-cat expression, sat by the back door looking trim and tidy.

"Anyone in?" I heard Mum call, and then she came through to the kitchen and put a bag of vegetables on the table.

"No, was the stern reply," she muttered to herself (it was one of her jokes). And then she saw me.

"Well! However did *you* get in?" she asked.

I put my head on one side and looked as pleasing and charming as possible. *"Miaow!"* I said. It came out as one of those cute, almost-silent miaows that cats do sometimes.

She bent to stroke me. "Aren't *you* a lovely boy!" she said. And then she looked at me hard. "Or girl, perhaps. Yes, I rather think you're a girl. You're too pretty to be a boy, aren't you?"

I moved my mouth whiskers slightly – the cat equivalent of a smile.

"My Tabitha likes cats – she'd love to see you!" Mum said, and she went to the bottom of the stairs and called up. "Tabitha! Are you around?"

She came back into the kitchen and looked up to the open window. "I suppose you got in there. He shouldn't have left it open." She looked over to the note and read it. "What *is* he going on about?" she muttered.

I rubbed myself against her legs.

"Want some milk, puss?"

I gave another half-silent miaow. Normally when I'm thirsty I'd rather drink anything but

83

milk, but as a cat I really fancied it.

"There you are," she said, putting a saucer-ful on the floor. "Drink it all up!"

I played my part to perfection, dipping my nose almost in the milk and lapping with my tongue. A funny process, actually: I never real-ized cats curl their tongue *backwards* when they lap – till I found myself doing it.

I drank about half, then stopped and licked the bits outside my mouth and put a quick paw around my face and whiskers to collect any extra droplets. I've seen cats do this many times, so I knew I looked adorable.

"*There's* a good puss!" Mum said, in the same voice she once used with Jamie and Sam when they'd finished up all their baby mush. She smiled at me. "You know what? You're like that cat that used to be at Aunt Mitzi's!"

I blinked. This was a bit too close for com-fort. Mum looked at me more closely. "Funny, you've even got that little extra tuft of hair just in front of your ears."

I blinked again, startled. *Had I?* I didn't know that, hadn't noticed.

She straightened up. "Perhaps you're a rel-ative," she mused, and then she turned away and started unpacking the vegetables.

I went to sit by the kitchen door and miaowed.

"Do you want to go out, then?"

"*Miaow!*"

She unlocked the door. "Off you go. Come and see me again!"

I miaowed to tell her that of course I'd see her again, because I was her daughter and lived there, and then I trotted out with my tail held high.

I went round to the front and into Mrs Neil-next-door's garden, where I couldn't resist pulling up a couple of the second-time-in plants, just for the fun of it.

There was a sudden furious banging on the front window, though, and I decided not to hang around. I nipped over her front wall and went down the street pretty niftily, and as I did so I heard the sound of a door being opened and then a *Whoosh!* as a bucket of water was thrown towards the place where I'd been digging a moment or two before.

Missed! I thought, and I carried on to the end of the road without further incident. At the top of Emily's road there was a brown paper bag in the gutter and I couldn't resist having a nose inside. But when I did, I found it contained a half-eaten orange, and I couldn't get my head out quickly enough. The thing is, as a girl, I quite like oranges.

I got to Emily's house and sat on her front wall while ballet music floated down to me from her open window. I just *had* to get to see her this time.

I decided that going to sit on her front step

would be a wise move, then if anyone came out of the door, I could slip in. Sure enough, after I'd only been there a few moments, the milkman pulled up in his van, came down the path and knocked.

He glanced at me and scowled. "What're you doing here? Clear off!" he muttered as he put three pints of milk down on the step.

I stared at him disdainfully. Everyone else thought I was beautiful! Besides, I had just as much right to be there as he did. He was obviously a dog person having a bad day.

Emily's mum opened the front door and they exchanged some chit-chat about the milk bill. I was just about to slip through and up the stairs when the milkman nodded at me in pretend admiration.

"Fine cat you got there!" he said. "New, is he?"

Emily's Mum looked at me, indignant at the notion that she might own a cat. "Never seen him before in my life! *Shoo!*" she said. "Get away!"

I had no intention of shooing. While she was putting away her purse I zipped through her legs and up the stairs to Emily's room.

"What're you … come back at once!" her mum shouted.

"Dead crafty, cats!" I heard the milkman say as he took his leave.

Emily's mum ran up the stairs. I miaowed

once at normal level outside Emily's room, then again, much louder.

Emily opened her bedroom door. She saw me and her jaw dropped.

"Shoo that cat out!" her mum said, coming up fast behind me. "The dirty thing just came in off the street."

I ran past Emily, into her room and under her bed.

"It ... it's OK," Emily said. "I ... I'll put it out in a minute."

"Don't be silly. What d'you want that in there for?"

"It's only a cat," Emily said. "It won't hurt." She began to close the door on her mum.

"Get it out!"

"In a minute."

"Emily! Remember you're allergic!" her mum cried as a parting shot.

Emily shut the door and locked it. As I came out from under the bed, she turned and looked at me sternly. "Now, you're not ... no, of course you're not," she said, and then she laughed self-consciously. "I'm talking to a cat! I must be mad."

CHAPTER TEN

"Miaow," I said. There was a lot in that miaow. It meant: Yes, it's me in here. See, I told you so, and now will you believe me?

"Nice pussy," Emily said cautiously.

I sat and stared at her.

"Just exploring, I expect, and you ran in here out of curiosity. As cats do."

I blinked.

"Just coincidence that – I mean, I mustn't think that just because you're a black cat—" She looked at me uneasily. "You're not – no … *ha ha* … as if."

She suddenly dropped on all fours in front of me and looked at me very hard, as if she was trying to see right inside me. "Tabitha?" she asked urgently. "Are you in there?" And then she gave a nervous laugh and jumped up again. "Honestly," she muttered, "here I am lying on the carpet trying to make conversation with a cat."

I got up and began to walk around the room, sniffing at things, looking for a way to prove human intelligence and show who I was. Wherever I walked, Emily watched me intently.

"Hungry, are you?" she asked. "Or d'you want something else? You don't … er … want to go *outside* do you?"

I ignored that and carried on prowling. The school project that we'd been working on was in a file by the side of her desk, and when I found it, I pawed it so that it fell over.

Emily watched me. "That's funny," she muttered.

Using my teeth and my paws, I pulled out the papers inside and found the title page: *Victorian Servants* by Emily Joseph and Tabitha Brown.

I put my paw onto my own name and looked up at her.

Her jaw dropped.

I began purring.

"No!" she breathed. "Coincidence. Or she's trained the cat and sent it round!"

I then dabbed my paw on my name several times, as if I was pointing at it.

Emily gasped and went quite pale. She made several efforts to speak and when she managed to, her voice came out all squeaky. "OK, then," she said, "if it *is* you …" she looked over her shoulder as if she thought she was being caught on one of those shows where they secretly film people, "... and I don't for one moment think it is, mind, then do something else."

"*Miaow?*" I said, which meant, like what?

"You must follow my instructions: jump on the bed and bring me my nightie."

"*Miaow,*" I said by way of protest. Really. I was a cat, not a performing seal.

"Go on, then," she urged.

I looked at her, then rolled over on my back and put my legs in the air as if wanting my tummy tickled.

She grinned, looking relieved. "Thank goodness! You're just a cat. That's all right, then. Of course, I knew you couldn't possibly—"

"*Miaow!*" I said, meaning, fooled you! And then I jumped up, ran across the room, sprang onto her bed, picked up the nightdress case in my teeth and dragged it back.

"No!" she said in a shocked voice. "I don't believe it! Just don't believe it! No!"

I yawned. How long was this going to go on?

"Is it really you, Tabitha?"

I miaowed.

"Really and truly?"

Getting bored with the whole thing, I turned my back on her and began to wash myself.

"OK, then," she said in a voice which said she supposed she had no alternative. "I believe you. OK, Tabitha."

I turned round to face her.

"But *honestly*..."

I was about to turn away again when she slipped off her chair and lay full length on the floor, next to me. Then she started. "How long have you been changed now? Do you feel strange? Do your legs get tangled up when you walk? What if you need to go to the loo? Are you hungry now? Do other cats look at you funny? What if—"

I let out a yowl of protest.

"I wish you could talk!" she said earnestly. "There are so many things I want to ask." And then she sneezed. "Blast!" she said. "I forgot – I'm allergic to cats and rabbits."

I rolled my eyes. Fat lot of good she was going to be as a best friend if she sneezed every time I got near her.

But I'd had an idea. I went over to our history project again and pulled out our rough notebook. Then I carried it over to Emily, and rolled over a pen.

"What?" she said. "Do you want to write me something? OK, then, have a go!"

I looked pointedly down at my feet as if to say that paws were never meant to hold pens.

"What, then?"

I pushed the pen towards her. She sneezed

91

on me and I jumped and backed away. The sneeze felt horrible: damp and very loud.

"You want *me* to write something?"

I twitched my whiskers.

"But you can hear me anyway."

I miaowed.

She looked at me hard. "You're trying to tell me something, aren't you?"

Oh, we are bright, I thought.

I miaowed again, then bent and tried to tear some pages out of the rough book.

"Let me think," she murmured. "You can't speak and I can. So we've got to find a way for you to, as well." There was another pause, then she said excitedly, "I get it! I get it!"

She tore out a double page, then folded it over and over and tore down the folds so that she had a pile of little squares of paper. "See. I'm not just a pretty face," she said, beginning to write the letters of the alphabet on the squares.

She arranged the letters in a long line all down the carpet.

"OK!" she said happily. "Let's go. Now, what do you feel like?"

I began to walk up and down the line, daintily touching each letter in turn with my right paw.

"Like a cat," Emily spelt out. "Yes. I suppose you do." She sneezed violently and there was a knock on her door.

"Emily! Is that cat still in there? I can hear you sneezing."

"Yes, it is but—"

"We're going out now. Open the door, will you?"

Raising her eyebrows at me meaningfully, Emily opened the door.

I lay down in a tame cat posture, my front paws doubled under me, my eyes half closed as if I was nearly asleep.

Her mother looked at me suspiciously, then transferred her attention to the pieces of paper. "What's all this mess for?"

"It's a project," Emily said.

Her mother looked at them. "I can't think what sort of a project involves writing down the letters of the alphabet," she said, "but you can tidy them all up now because we're going out. We're meeting Gran in town."

"Oh, Mum!" Emily protested.

"Don't pretend you've forgotten," her mum said. She moved towards me. "Let's get this animal out. Come on, Tiddles!"

I glowered at her.

"Leave her. I'll put her out," Emily said.

"No, you won't. Your eyes are streaming already!" And before I could move, Emily's mum pounced on me, grabbing me under my front legs and holding me so that my back legs dangled in a most undignified way.

"Careful!" Emily said.

"Get your shoes on," said her mum, carrying me down the stairs and almost bashing my head on the bannisters.

She opened the front door and literally threw me out.

"Off you go!" she said. "Scram!"

I flew through the air, landed on the grass and ran straight under a bush in the garden, needing to hide for a moment to restore my injured pride. Not only had I been called Tiddles, but I'd been dangled, had all the air squashed out of me and been chucked out of the house.

I did some deep breathing, and after I'd breathed enough, I carefully washed my face and paws. After that I jumped over the wall and ran home without looking back. I'd never really liked Emily's mum.

I didn't want to risk being seen by my own mum again, so I ran straight up the tree outside and in through my bedroom window. Sinking onto my cushion, I fell asleep for an instant and woke again.

I stretched, went into the bathroom for a glass of water and then went downstairs. I knew that Mum was in the sitting-room watching football on TV, so I went into the kitchen, opened and shut the back door loudly and then went through to her.

"Oh, there you are!" Mum said. "On your own? I thought you'd gone out with the boys."

I shook my head. "I've been round to Emily's."

"It's a pity you weren't in earlier," she said, "because when I came home that nice black cat was in here – the one I saw on the wall the other day."

I tried to look drop-dead amazed. "*Was* it?"

"Such a lovely cat, sitting in the kitchen, quite at home."

"Oh. Perhaps it's adopted us."

She got up and looked out of the window. "You'd like it. You didn't see it outside anywhere just now, did you?"

I joined her at the window and we looked up and down the road. "No. It must have gone again," I said. "What a pity."

Later, after I'd explained to Mum about the two pound coins and taken possession of them, Dad, the twins and a whole lot of carrier bags came back from the shops. Not only did Jamie and Sam have new trainers, but they also had matching T-shirts and hooded tops.

I felt bitter and twisted about this – it was months since I'd had any new clothes – but I soon felt better when the twins went up to their room and discovered their cars.

They were down again in a flash, shouting to Mum, Dad and anyone who'd listen about cars that moved, locked doors, mysterious noises and *X-Files*-type happenings.

I looked only faintly interested. "Oh, come on," I said. "If your door really *was* locked, then one of you must be playing a trick on the other. That's all there is to it."

They glared at each other and there was a brief tussle.

"Hang on a sec," I said. "Were the cars in any particular place – or shape?"

"Why d'you want to know?" Sam asked suspiciously.

"They were in a sort of X," Jamie said.

I gave a short, false gasp of amazement. "An X! Oh my god, X marks the spot! The mysterious occult X shape!"

"Whassa *cult*?" Jamie asked.

"Magic … spooky."

"Stuff and nonsense!" said Dad. "Don't go filling their heads with rubbish, Tabitha."

I shrugged. "'Course. That's all it is." I lowered my voice. "It doesn't mean your bedroom is *haunted* or anything…"

CHAPTER ELEVEN

"Roast goose with stuffing," I muttered in amazement, staring at the tins of cat food. "Pork and turkey, beef hotpot, lamb in jelly, liver and kidney, turkey with roast vegetables." My voice rose to a squeal: "Seafood platter!"

"Do you want some help, dear?"

I turned away from the piles and miles of tins to the assistant who was standing beside me and eyeing me very oddly. "No, I was just … er … looking."

"Looking at the cat food?"

I smiled uneasily. "I'm doing a school project," I said. You could get away with murder with those two words.

"I see, dear," she said. "Well, do carry on."

I carried on looking at the ten lines of cats on bright labels, with ten times ten standing behind *them*. I was looking at a whole army of cats consuming a whole zoo-ful of other animals: cows, ducks, geese, rabbits, lambs – and probably llama and lion, if you looked hard enough.

Feeling slightly queasy, I moved up the aisle a bit to where the more expensive, gourmet ("Doesn't your cat deserve it?") food was. There was also special food for cats with dainty digestions, tinned milk for kittens and a huge variety of cat biscuits. These I quite liked the look of. They might seem a bit dry and boring, but they would also be nicely free of the gristle, jelly and tubes I just knew were packed into the tinned stuff. If I ever stayed a cat for a long time, then these were what I'd go for, I decided. And such nice shapes, too – including a variety which contained "real rabbit flavour". *Real* rabbit flavour? I puzzled. From real rabbits, I supposed. But what were imitation ones?

I gazed at a packet of sardine-shaped, salmon pink and salmon flavour biscuits. Perhaps, I thought, I ought to keep a few crunchy snacks around the place. They could be in a bowl under my bed and if, as a cat, I got a bit peckish, then I could have a nibble. It seemed like a good idea, just like the cat equivalent of a packet of salt and vinegar crisps, so I put them in my basket.

I moved on to cat incidentals: velvet flea collars, vitamin tablets, cat bowls and chocolate buttons for good cats. Then I came to cat litter, where I stood for ages in front of a stack of shiny bags, each showing a very smart black cat with a blue bow round its neck.

Black cats, I decided, had the shiniest fur, the greenest eyes, the perkiest ears with the pinkest insides. Black cats were undoubtedly the cat's whiskers.

I'd just thought this and was smiling at my own wit when I realized someone was shaking my arm.

"Here you are!" Emily said.

I nodded.

"I believe you now!"

"I should think so," I said.

"Sorry I didn't at first. It was a bit much to take in, though."

I smiled graciously.

"But what are you doing here in the pet food section?"

"Nothing!"

"You looked really *soppy*. You were just staring at those packets of cat litter and smiling to yourself."

"I wasn't." I shrugged her off. "I was just … looking at things. Shopping."

"You weren't going to buy anything, were you? Not any cat things? I mean, talk about a giveaway!"

"'Course not," I said.

She looked down at my basket. "You were!

You've got cat biscuits. You can't take home cat biscuits! What would your mum say?"

"Oh," I sighed. "All right." I walked over and put the biscuits back. "I just thought it would be nice to keep a snack indoors."

"What – in case any cat mates drop by?"

"Ha ha," I said. "Anyway, I was only looking because I'm interested in cat things. What's wrong with that? You're interested in ballet stuff, I'm interested in cat stuff."

Emily hurried me down the pet aisle and towards the checkouts. "Your mum told me I'd find you in here. She said you went out an hour and a half ago to get one or two things for her."

"I was only looking round a bit," I said, niggled. "I didn't realize there was a time limit!"

As we waited in the checkout queue Emily nudged me, her eyes bright. "Have you … *you know* … again?"

I shook my head. "No, not yet. I don't lose my temper every day of my life."

"So it's always then, is it? When you get into a paddy?"

"I *think* so," I said. I lowered my voice slightly. "It seems to be when I lose control. Somehow I just slip out of being a girl and slip into being a cat."

"And will it go on happening all the time now, d'you think?" she asked excitedly. "For ever?"

100

"I don't know," I said, shrugging. "How can I tell? I've got no one to ask."

"Didn't your aunt say anything else to you that day? Nothing else at all?"

"I can't remember," I said.

I'd been thinking and thinking about that, about whether Aunt Mitzi had dropped any other hints. I'd even wondered whether it was worth asking Mum if we could go back to the little house in Somerset so I could look for clues. I'd thought lots about the day we'd visited, and how I'd seen the cat in the garden, and then later when Aunt Mitzi had appeared. If only I'd known at the time how important that day, that meeting, was going to be, I'd have taken more notice of what had been happening.

I paid for Mum's stuff and we went out. We were halfway down the high street, Emily cross-examining me all the way, before I thought of something.

"Oh, blast! Mutton!" I said. "He's tied up outside the supermarket."

We wheeled around and started back. "I didn't think you liked him," Emily said. "Why d'you bring him with you?"

"Mum made me. The twins weren't up and she said he needed a walk."

As we approached the supermarket, Mutton saw me and started whining and pulling away.

"Why's he doing that?"

"Because he doesn't like me now," I said. "He was doing that all the way here."

Emily's jaw dropped. "D'you think he knows, then?"

"Dunno," I shrugged. "Maybe. If dogs are that smart."

Mutton was straining on his lead, trying to get as far away from me as possible. The nearer I got, the more he whined, leapt and yelped.

Two women went by, looking at me strangely.

"It's really embarrassing," I said to Emily as I undid Mutton's lead. "People must think I'm ill-treating him."

"I'll take him," she said, and when she took the lead Mutton immediately quietened down. He moved as far away from me as the lead would allow, though, and walked home slightly sideways, keeping his eye on me all the time.

"I was thinking," Emily said as we set off again, "that we need to devise some sort of way of talking for you, for when you, *you know*."

"We've got the alphabet," I said.

"Yes, but I can't keep getting twenty-six pieces of paper out of my pocket and putting them on the ground, can I? We need a quick method of working out what you want to do, otherwise I'm never going to know. Suppose I start doing something you don't like?"

"I could bite you," I suggested.

"Oh, very funny."

Outside the house, the twins were sitting on the wall waiting for Mutton.

"Why have you got him?" Sam demanded.

"He doesn't like *you*," said Jamie.

"The feeling," I said, "is completely mutual."

"So why did you take him?"

"If you must know, Mum told me I had to," I said.

Emily handed over the lead and we went towards the house. Behind us we heard, "Tabitha Brown went to town, and her bum went round and round!"

"You've got a fat bum!" Sam yelled as an afterthought, and they both guffawed with laughter.

I raised my eyebrows at Emily. "Excuse my brothers' sophisticated humour."

We went into my bedroom, where Emily walked round the cushion respectfully, as if at any moment it might leap at her and bite her ankles.

"I've been thinking," she said. "Couldn't we do something special with this – whatever you call it – this power of yours?"

"Like what?"

"Well, we could go on telly or something. We could do an act where you spell out words.

We could be famous: the amazing Emily and her cat."

"Shouldn't that be the amazing cat and her Emily?"

"Well, whatever. We'd be famous!" she said. "We'd have a travelling show, go all over the world and earn lots of money. We'd be rich and we could buy big houses for our families." She looked round. "This house is quite small for all you lot, isn't it? This bedroom's tiny!"

"Ah, I'm working on that," I said, and I told her about the tricks I'd played on the twins and how now, for some unaccountable reason, they thought that their bedroom was haunted. "Do me a favour," I said. "If you see them again before you go home, say something about hearing weird noises coming from their bedroom, will you?"

She promised to. "And will you think about my travelling show idea, then?"

"How can I?" I said. "How could I guarantee changing right on cue each time? Just think – the television cameras would be waiting to roll and someone would announce, "Emily and her Amazing Cat!" and then out would come Emily and her not-very-amazing friend."

Her face fell. But she couldn't think of a way of guaranteeing that I'd change, either.

"I've been thinking about something else, too," she went on after a moment. "What if only a bit of you changed? What if something

104

went wrong halfway and you ended up with the top half of a girl and the bottom half of a cat!"

I looked at her. "Oh, thanks a lot," I said. "It's nice to have something else to worry about."

"You'd be like a mermaid. A catmaid! Or perhaps you'd be left with just a bit of cat. Whiskers, say, or a tail." She smiled brightly. "If it was a tail you could probably hide it quite well – tuck it in your knickers."

"And I suppose if it was ears, I could hide them under a woolly hat," I said.

She had to go home shortly after that, and as she went down our front path I waved to her from my bedroom window. By the gate, the twins jumped out on her from behind a bush, but she said something to them and they seemed to lose a bit of bounce. As she crossed the road she glanced up at me and gave me a brief thumbs-up sign.

I spent the afternoon going through old photographs of Mum's family, going out to Mum in the garden every few minutes to ask her who was who, and what year she thought it was, then writing it on the back of the photo. The striking family likeness between Mum's granny, Aunt Mitzi (who was her daughter, of course) and me was spooky – I'd never really noticed it before. I didn't look anything like

Mum had looked when she was a girl, but uncannily like an old, faded photograph of Aunt Mitzi taken when she was about twelve.

When I looked into dates I discovered a strange thing: that Aunt Mitzi's own mum had lived to be a really old, old lady, so when Mum had spoken about remembering a cat being at Aunt Mitzi's when she'd once visited her, *Aunt Mitzi's mum had still been alive*. That seemed to mean that the power could pass on any time – not just on the death of the person who had it. But if so, how did that person know when it was time to pass it on to someone else? Did it just transfer on its own?

While I was wondering about this, I found something quite exciting. It was a large photograph of a family group at a wedding, posed in a garden. Mum was there, really young, the man getting married was her brother, my Uncle John, and I recognized several other aunts and uncles. Granny was there, too, and Grandad, but there was no sign of Aunt Mitzi, even though she was in another photo of the same wedding group outside a church. What *was* there in the garden shot, though, sitting in front of the bride, was a very upright, sleek and gleaming-coated black cat.

A black cat for luck. But how many people at the wedding knew that the black cat must have been Aunt Mitzi?

CHAPTER TWELVE

"Per-lease!" Mum arrived on the upstairs landing heaving with crossness and exasperation. "Stop this shouting, Tabitha!" She poked the three of us in turn. "I want you neat and clean, I want you well-behaved, and I want you quiet. Is that *too* much to ask?"

My hands, which had been reaching out to knock Jamie and Sam's heads together, reluctantly fell to my sides.

"Now, you *know* what a stickler Granny Brown is," Mum went on, "and I don't want to give her any cause for complaint. We've all got to spend a whole day in her company and, believe me, it's twice as bad for me as it is for you."

Mum pulled me under the light and looked at me more closely. "What *have* you done to yourself, Tabitha? Been smearing yourself with coal dust? Go back in the bathroom and wash properly."

The twins snorted with laughter.

"I *have* washed," I protested. "It's—"

"Honestly! I thought it was only the twins I had to remind about personal hygiene."

"Mum!" I protested. "They put this soap in the bathroom. Black-face soap! That's what I was having a go at them about."

Mum tutted. "I can't believe you'd fall for something as idiotic as that, Tabitha."

"We were only *resting* it in there," Sam said between sniggers. "You weren't supposed to use it."

I gave him a push – quite a light one – and he immediately fell to the floor, whimpering.

"Now look what you've done!" Mum said.

"I hardly touched him! He's putting it on!"

"That's enough, Tabitha! Just go and wash your face, get dressed and then come downstairs. I want you – all three of you – sitting quietly reading when Granny Brown comes. I want your faces clean, your bedrooms tidy, I want the dog out of the way, I want peace. PEACE AND QUIET!" she roared.

I went into the bathroom, counting to ten. I was very angry, but it was manageable. I really couldn't do with changing at the moment; things were hectic enough with the imminent arrival of Granny Brown.

She was Dad's mum, and a bit of an old trout. Dad had been brought up very, very strictly (or so he said) and Granny Brown thought we were out of control in comparison. This was why Mum was so stressed out; a visit from Granny Brown meant wall-to-wall aggro.

With their immaculate timing, the twins had chosen this morning to play their latest stupid trick on me: black-face soap. I'm usually on the lookout for things like that and I don't know why I didn't catch on, but they'd got a soap which almost exactly matched our usual one and I was in a rush. I'd washed with it and not realized what had happened until I'd looked in the mirror to brush my hair. It was at that moment that I'd heard the enemy chanting, "Tabitha Brown – her face is brown!" and rushed out to splat them. The row that followed had brought Mum upstairs.

I washed my face again, using some of Mum's moisturiser to get the last smudgy bits of black off, and then I went back into my bedroom to get dressed. While I was dressing I did some deep breathing and gave myself a strict talking-to about losing my cool. I made an agreement with myself that on this day I'd be tantrum and temper-free, so that in comparison the twins would be shown up as the hateful little beasts they truly were. And if Mum didn't realize it, then at least Granny Brown might.

I finished getting dressed and, in my efforts

to be perfect, went downstairs and out to the garden shed to clean my shoes. Mutton, removed to the garden for the day, set up a long, low whine on seeing me, but I ignored him.

I was halfway through polishing the first shoe, trying to think pleasant thoughts all the time, when I heard a thump and a click, then the sound of someone running away.

I jumped up immediately and tried the door but knew, of course, that it was locked. *And* who had locked it.

"Come back!" I shouted, but I heard the distant sound of our back door being closed and realized that he – *they* – had gone inside.

I shook the shed door and shouted. The shed was a fair way down the garden, though, and Mum was probably wafting around the dining-room at the front of the house, poised for Granny Brown's arrival.

I gritted my teeth, fumed, bit my lip. Probably, at this very moment, Granny Brown was entering the dining-room, examining surfaces for dust and asking what brand of tea she was going to be served. Mum would be calling up the stairs for me, then asking the twins if they knew where I was, and *they* would be pretending to look for me and then reporting that I'd disappeared. Mum would be preparing dire punishments...

I shouted again, good intentions forgotten,

and shook the door. When this didn't do anything, I kicked at it with both feet in turn. After this, losing it altogether and bursting with fury, I picked up a wooden crate to use as a battering ram. It was then that I felt myself beginning to change...

I hastily put down the box and waited – waited for the slow, soft sensation to sweep over my body and the calm, contented feeling to slip into my mind, and a few moments later I was padding softly and silently across the grass towards the house.

It had been a bit of a struggle getting out of the small top window, because the shelf I'd used before was now crammed with flowerpots. But I'd managed it, squeezing through a space much less than the width of my whiskers.

I ran round to the front of the house (Granny Brown's car was standing in the roadway) and began to climb the tree up to my bedroom window so I could change back.

"Psst!"

Awkwardly, my head at a funny angle, I looked down to see Emily standing by our wall.

"Is that you, Tabitha?" she hissed. "What are you doing?"

I gave a hurried *miaow* as much as to say, Isn't that obvious?

"Why don't you come home with me? We

can go for a walk or something."

I was clinging with my claws in the bark all this time, not quite sure whether to carry on up the tree or go back down and have a word with her.

"Guess what? I've just been into town and there's a cat show tomorrow. I was wondering if…"

I heard the noise of our front door being opened.

"Emily!" Mum called urgently. "Emily, have you seen Tabitha?"

I lost my grip and half-ran/half-fell down the tree, managing to turn awkwardly at the last minute.

"Er … well…" Emily said, giving me a side-long, panicky glance.

Feeling a bit ruffled after my undignified fall, I faked disinterest and stared in the other direction.

"She's disappeared! I've just rung your house to see if she was there."

"I … er…"

"I'm going to kill her when I see her – going off like this when her granny's here," Mum said. "If you see her, tell her to come in straight away, will you?"

Emily nodded, eyes wide.

Mum turned to go in, then noticed me. "Oh, it's that cat again," she said. "Has it followed you? Does it belong to someone in your road?"

Emily looked dumb. "Don't know," she said.

Mum gave her a funny look and went in. Emily bent to stroke me. "You heard," she said. "You're to go in straight away."

"*Miaow!*"

I ran up the tree and looked down to see her watching me admiringly as I leapt across to the windowsill and balanced daintily all the way along. I went in through my bedroom window, had reached my cushion and was just turning round and round on it, working the material under my paws and getting comfortable, when I realized I had something stuck to my side: a sticky label.

I managed to get it off with my paw. It was the label from a bottle of garden pesticide, and I must somehow have picked it up in the shed. It was bordered in black, with DANGER! written across the top and a stark skull and crossbones underneath.

I stared at it. This was just too good not to make use of, so I put off transmogrifying for a moment. I carefully picked up the label in my teeth, went out of my window and into the twins' room.

I patted their cars into a rough circle and put the label down flat in the centre of it so they'd see it as soon as they came in. To make things even more baffling and spooky, on my way out I tugged their curtains shut, so that it would be almost dark in there when they found the warning sign.

And then I went straight into my own room and curled up on my cushion...

"Really, I can't think where Tabitha's got to," I heard Mum saying as I came down the stairs. "She was so looking forward to seeing you, too."

I heard Granny Brown sniff.

"Are you sure you've looked properly, boys?"

"We've looked everywhere!" Jamie said. "And our room's locked, so she's not in there."

"She must have gone out!" Sam piped up.

"Yes, it's a bit rude of her, isn't it?" Jamie added piously, and I pictured the two of them sitting side by side on the sofa, scrubbed and shiny, pictures of innocent boyhood.

"I just can't..." Mum began again, and then I walked in.

The expressions on the twins' faces – well, I reckon it was worth one of my nine lives just to see them.

"You couldn't..." Sam began, going pale.

"How did...?" Jamie stuttered.

"Where have you *been*?" said Mum.

I thought about dropping the twins in it, but decided to save that for later. "Sorry, Mum. Unavoidably detained," I said.

I went over to Granny Brown and kissed her lavishly. "Hello, Gran," I said. "Sorry I wasn't here when you arrived. I was just ... er ... taking a catnap."

CHAPTER THIRTEEN

"Well, I'm really not sure…" I said. "I like my little room. I don't want to change."

"Oh, *pleeeease*," Jamie said.

"Oh, Tab, be a sport!" said Sam.

"We'll do anything, won't we?" Jamie said, nudging Sam.

"We'll do jobs for you for a month!"

I shook my head. "I don't know. My room's small, but it's cosy. And so peaceful … and unhaunted," I murmured.

This set up fresh whines, squeals and promises to be nice to me for a year and do jobs for me for six months if I'd *only*…

"I'll think about it," I said, and went back in my own bedroom and started to pack.

I'd enjoyed a delicious revenge for the shed incident the previous afternoon when, on Granny Brown's departure, the twins had gone up to their room and discovered the puzzling and mysterious secret sign. I was completely in the clear, because there was no way I could have got in through their locked door. The other good thing was that finding a mysterious secret sign in their room had driven out of their heads any questions about just how I'd managed to get out of the shed.

They had started trying to persuade me to change rooms immediately and though I'd been deeply against it at first, I was slowly allowing myself to be talked round. Mum said the whole idea of changing rooms was ridiculous (she didn't buy the haunted idea, saying that one twin must be playing tricks on the other) and the twins would be much too cramped in my room, but if we wanted to do it we were just to get on and leave her out of it.

By three o'clock that afternoon I was in my new lovely big room, admiring my acres of space and planning what I was going to do with it. Moving had been surprisingly easy and had just involved a lot of piling, shoving, carrying and pushing. The twins' beds, luckily, were bunk beds, so fitted on top of each other, and Jamie and Sam were now on the other side of the wall, knee-deep in cars and rubbish. Everyone was happy.

While I was nailing up my ethnic wall hanging and deciding where I was going to put my posters, Emily arrived.

"You managed it!" she said, looking round at all the gorgeous space. "You crafty thing!"

"Ssshhh!"

I filled her in on the shed and sticky label incident and she goggled and marvelled a bit, then flopped on my bed, fanning herself to cool down. "I'm just about dying of embarrassment," she said. "Tell me this, have you — *you know* — today?"

I shook my head.

"I thought as much. So I've just had a long conversation with Tibby from number thirty-six."

I giggled.

"It's not funny," she said. "There was a black cat sitting on the wall outside my house and naturally I thought it was you, so I sat down next to it and started chatting."

I grinned. "Did it say anything interesting?"

She shook her head. "No, it didn't," she said. "Worse than that, while I was sitting there making polite conversation with it, two boys from school saw me and said they were going to ring someone and get me taken away." She put her head in her hands and groaned.

There was a scratching at the bedroom door, then a yelp.

"That's Mutton," I said. "He hasn't caught on that we've changed rooms." I went to the door. "I'll just give him a reminder."

I opened the door and Mutton, who'd been wagging his tail eagerly, gave a start at the sight of me and backed off with an alarmed whine.

"See!" I said to him. "You daft dog! *I'm* in here now – and Jamie and Sam are in *there*!" And I thumped their door for them to let him in.

I shut mine. "That's the fourth time," I said to Emily. "Dogs, eh? When it comes to working things out they aren't a patch on cats."

I passed Emily a pile of books to put on my new, spacious bookshelves and then picked up the old photograph of the wedding group which I'd borrowed from the photo box and found a frame for. I was going to nail it in pride of place, just above the new space I'd earmarked for the velvet cushion.

"Have a look at this," I said. "What can you see?"

Emily looked. "It's just some old-fashioned wedding," she said. "Hey, is that girl in the front your mum?"

I nodded.

"God, look at her hair!"

"See anything else?"

"Dunno. Just a lot of old fogies all wearing their best gear."

"Look at the cat!"

Her jaw dropped. "No! Is that *you*?"

"Not exactly," I said. "It's sort of my ancestor cat, though. It's Aunt Mitzi. She should be in the photograph, but she's not. Something must have made her cross at the reception!"

"Wow!" Emily said, marvelling and looking intently at the photograph.

I nodded, and started to tell her my theory on the power passing through the generations, dead or alive, but we both got a bit muddled over aunts, great-aunts and grannies and in the end Emily got bored and started telling me about her latest ballet exam. After that she pirouetted around the room and offered to give me lessons so we could do an act together: Emily and Her Amazing Dancing Cat.

By the time she went home I'd more or less got my things sorted. I went to the front gate with her and promised faithfully that next time I changed I'd go and see her, day or night, no matter what.

When I came back to the house, Mum was on the phone.

"Oh, that's lovely," she was saying. "First grandchild, eh? I'm thrilled for you. Just a sec…"

"It's your Uncle John," she said to me, beaming. "Julia's had her baby. A big one, too – nine pounds twelve ounces!"

As we don't do pounds and ounces at school this didn't mean a thing to me, but I tried to look impressed.

"It's a girl, but they haven't decided on a name yet."

I made suitable noises and was just going to carry on up the stairs when Mum said into the phone, "*Has* she? Are you sure? Babies usually have blue…"

I backtracked. "What?" I asked.

"Uncle John says the baby's got green eyes but I think he's just being fanciful." I could hear the murmur of Uncle John's voice and then Mum laughed. "Oh, really?"

"What?"

"He says she's got an absolute mop of jet-black hair!"

I sat down on the nearest stair.

"And that she's the image of you as a baby!"

"Oh," I said. *Oh*…

I closed my eyes while things worked themselves through my head. *Here* was the person I could pass the cushion to. When the time was right, when I *decided* the time was right, then I would pass on the power – and the cushion as a symbol of it. I knew it was up to me to decide whether to keep the power for ten years or for twenty years or for ever, or just until the new baby was a bit older.

I sat on the stairs and waited until Mum had finished getting details of where to send flowers and stuff like that, and then I said to send Julia my love.

"Can we visit her?" I asked when Mum

came off the phone.

"Your cousin Julia? Whatever for?"

"It's not so much her as the baby," I said.

"You've never taken any interest in babies before! What is it – a school project?"

"Something like that," I said. I wanted to see the baby, and I wanted to hold it. I knew I had to. It was my turn to be the fairy at the christening.

Mum phoned Uncle John back and arranged it, and I wandered upstairs, smiling to myself. One day I would pass on the cushion and the power.

But in the meantime – just as good old Aunt Mitzi had done – I was going to enjoy myself.

THE BEAST OF WHIXALL MOSS
Pauline Fisk

At the age of eleven, Jack is resigned to his world.

So what if he can never satisfy his mother's desire for perfection and his brother can? So what if he's lonely out on Whixall Moss? He doesn't care – or so he likes to tell himself. Then one day he sees, in a boat hidden on the creek, a beautiful, fabulous beast. At once he is filled with a wild longing: he must own it. But the boat's mysterious inhabitants have other ideas...

Gripping and powerful, this novel by Smarties Book Prize Winner Pauline Fisk is a tale that will live long in the imagination.

LONE WOLF
Kristine L. Franklin

Three years ago, following a family tragedy, Perry and his dad left the city and moved to a remote cabin in the woods. Perry spends much of his time with his dog, Rhonda, in the cave that's his secret hideout. Then goofy, inquisitive Willow Pestalozzi and her large family move into the empty house nearby and Perry finds himself having to face things he's tried so hard to forget…

Kristine L. Franklin's tender, moving story reveals how learning to laugh again also means being able, at last, to cry.

MONKEY
Veronica Bennett

"Hey, Pritchard! Monkey-features! Monkey, monkey, monkey!"

By teenager Harry Pritchard's own admission, he's a dork. At school he's taunted and bullied by the vicious "Brigadier" Gerard Fox; at home he's weighed down by the chores his mother sets him – the worst of which is having to look after his irritating little sister, Emma. At least, that *was* the worst until Mum volunteers him to visit a severely disabled patient of hers, Simon Schofield, two evenings a week. She says it'll do him good. But how can being a helpless cripple's monkey help him end Brig's bullying? Or get him a part in the Drama Club play? Or win the attentions of beautiful Louise Harding, the girl of his dreams? Simon, though, turns out to be quite different from what Harry imagines and, after meeting him, Harry's life undergoes dramatic – and traumatic – changes!

Touching, perceptive and thought-provoking, Veronica Bennett's book is a first novel of outstanding assurance and quality.

FIRE, BED AND BONE
Henrietta Branford

The year is 1381 and unrest is spreading like plague.

England's peasants are tired of the hardship and injustice they suffer at the hands of harsh landlords. Rebellion is in the air, bringing dramatic and violent upheaval to the lives of families like Rufus, Comfort and their children – and even to dogs, like the old hunting bitch who is the narrator of this unforgettable tale.

This gripping and vivid story by a Smarties Book Prize-winning author is an extraordinary achievement, depicting the tumult and tragedy of the Peasants' Revolt through the eyes, ears and nose of a dog.

MORE WALKER PAPERBACKS
For You to Enjoy